Serena Turned Her Fear Into Anger

"If you read your brochure, you'll see that your passage fee doesn't include your pick of the crew."

"Certain things have no price, Serena."

Something in his tone made her tremble. It was as if he'd already put his mark on her, a mark she wouldn't easily erase. "Stay away from me," she warned.

"No," Justin said mildly. "I've already dealt the cards, and the odds always favor the house."

"Well, I'm not interested," she hissed. "So deal me out."

Justin jingled the change in his pocket and smiled. "Not a chance."

NORA ROBERTS

lives with her two sons in the Blue Ridge Mountains of western Maryland. To be a published author is the lifetime dream she has seen fulfilled in the many books that she has written for Silhouette. Renowned for her warm characters and wit, Nora Roberts is a favorite with readers of romance.

Dear Reader:

Romance readers have been enthusiastic about Silhouette Special Editions for years. And that's not by accident: Special Editions were the first of their kind and continue to feature realistic stories with heightened romantic tension.

The longer stories, sophisticated style, greater sensual detail and variety that made Special Editions popular are the same elements that will make you want to read book after book.

We hope that you enjoy this Special Edition today, and will enjoy many more.

The Editors at Silhouette Books

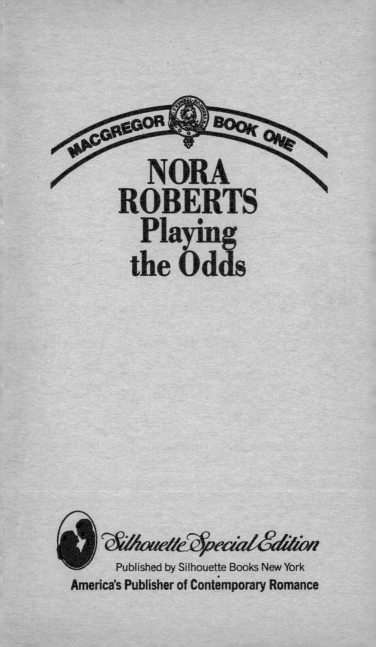

MACGREGOR · BOOK ONE

NORA ROBERTS
Playing the Odds

Silhouette Special Edition

Published by Silhouette Books New York

America's Publisher of Contemporary Romance

SILHOUETTE BOOKS
300 East 42nd St., New York, N.Y. 10017

Copyright © 1985 by Nora Roberts

ISBN: 0-373-48208-6

First Silhouette Books printing March 1985
Second Silhouette Books printing February 1987

America's Publisher of Contemporary Romance

Printed in the U.S.A.

NORA ROBERTS

Available now, Nora Roberts's award-winning MacGregor series—*Playing the Odds*, *Tempting Fate*, *All the Possibilities*, and *One Man's Art*. If you missed any of them, we're proud to bring them all back in a special Collectors Edition.

One reader sums up what many of you have written and told us: "How I would love to read the love story of Daniel MacGregor as a young man first meeting and winning his wife!" Now, in Special Editions, we are happy to give you that story in *For Now, Forever*. It takes you back to the beginning and concludes the series in one exciting book. Each story stands on its own, but together they form a unique and wonderful family portrait. Don't miss them!

For Jason—the gambler

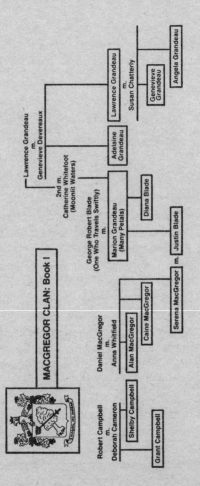

MACGREGOR CLAN: Book I

Robert Campbell
m.
Deborah Cameron

- Shelby Campbell
- Grant Campbell

Daniel MacGregor
m.
Anna Whitfield

- Alan MacGregor
- Caine MacGregor
- Serena MacGregor m. Justin Blade

Lawrence Grandeau
m.
Genevieve Devereaux

2nd m.
Catherine Whitefoot
(Moonlit Waters)

George Robert Blade
(One Who Travels Swiftly)
m.
Marion Grandeau
(Many Petals)

- Diana Blade
- Justin Blade

Adelaine Grandeau

Lawrence Grandeau
m.
Susan Chatterly

- Genevieve Grandeau
- Angela Grandeau

Chapter One

There was always a great deal of confusion, more noise, and a touch of panic to flavor the arrival of embarking passengers. Some were already a bit travel weary from their flight into Miami, others were running on the adrenaline of anticipation. The huge white ocean liner, the *Celebration*, waited in port—their ticket to fun, relaxation, romance. When they crossed the gangway, they would no longer be accountants, assistant managers, or teachers, but pampered passengers assured of being fed, spoiled, and entertained for the next ten days. The brochures guaranteed it.

From the rail of the Observation deck, Serena watched the flow of humanity. At that distance she could enjoy the color and noise, which never lost its appeal for her, without being caught in the inevitable tangle of fifteen hundred people trying to get to the same place at the same time. The cooks, the bartenders, the cabin stewards, had already begun the orgy of work that would continue, virtually uninterrupted, for the next ten days. But she had time. Serena relished it.

These were her idle moments—before the ship pulled out of port. She could remember her first experience with a cruise liner. She'd been eight, the youngest of the three children of financial wizard Daniel MacGregor and Dr. Anna Whitefield Mac-Gregor. There had been first-class cabins, where the steward had served her hot buns and juice in bed. Serena had enjoyed it the same way she enjoyed her tiny cabin in the crew's quarters now. They were both an adventure.

Serena remembered, too, the day she had told her parents of her plans to apply for a job with the *Celebration*. Her father had huffed and puffed about her throwing away her education. The more he had huffed, the more pronounced his soft Scottish burr had become. A woman who had graduated from Smith at the tender age of twenty, who had then gone on to earn degrees in English, history, and sociology didn't swab decks. And even as Serena had assured him that wasn't her intention, her mother had laughed, telling Daniel to let the child be. Because at six foot three and two hundred and twenty pounds, Daniel MacGregor was helpless against what he called his females, he did just that.

So Serena had gotten her job and had escaped from what had become endless years of study. She'd traded her three-room suite in the family mansion in Hyannis Port for a one-room broom closet with a bunk on a floating hotel. None of her coworkers cared what her

I.Q. was, or how many degrees she'd earned. They didn't know her father could have bought the cruise line lock, stock, and barrel if he'd had the whim, or that her mother was an authority on thoracic surgery. They didn't know her oldest brother was a senator and the younger a state's attorney. When they looked at her, they saw Serena. That was all she wanted.

Lifting her head, she let the wind take her hair. It danced on the breeze, a mass of blond, the rich shade of gold one found in old paintings. She had high, slanting cheekbones and a sharp, stubborn jaw. Her skin refused to tan, remaining a delicate peach to contrast with the violet-blue of her eyes. Her father called them purple; a few romantics had called them violet. Serena stubbornly termed them blue and left it at that. Men were drawn to them because of their uniqueness, then to her because of the elegant sexuality she exuded without thought. But she wasn't very interested.

Intellectually, Serena thought a man was a fool if he fell for a shade of irises. It was a matter of genetics after all, and had little to do with her personally. She'd listened to accolades on her eyes for twenty-six years with a kind of detached wonder. There was a miniature in her father's library of his great-great-grandmother, another Serena. If anyone had asked, she could have explained the process of genetics that resulted in the resemblance, down to the bone structure and eye shade—and the reputed temper. But the men she met were generally not interested in a scientific explanation, and Serena was generally not interested in them.

Below her, the crowd flowing up the gangway was

thinning. Shortly the calypso band would be playing on
the Lido deck to entertain the passengers while the ship
prepared to sail. Serena would enjoy staying outside,
listening to the tinny, rhythmic music and laughter.
There would be a buffet laden with more food than the
well over one thousand people could possibly eat,
exotic drinks, and excitement. Soon the rails would be
packed with people wanting that last glimpse of shore
before all there would be was open sea.

Wistfully, she watched the last stragglers come on
board. It was the final cruise of the season. When they
returned to Miami, the *Celebration* would go into dry
dock for two months. When it sailed again, Serena
wouldn't be on it. She'd already made up her mind that
it was time to move on. When she'd taken the job on
the ship, she had been looking for one thing—freedom
from years of study, from family expectations, from her
own restlessness. She knew she had accomplished
something in the year on her own. Serena had found
the independence she had always struggled for, and she
had escaped the niche so many of her college friends
had been determinedly heading for: a good marriage.

And yet, though she'd found the freedom and independence, she hadn't found the most important ingre-
dient: the goal. What did Serena MacGregor want to
do with the rest of her life? She didn't want the political
career both her brothers had chosen. She didn't want to
teach or lecture. She wanted excitement and challenges
and no longer wanted to look for them in a classroom.
They were all negative answers, but she knew whatever
it was that would fill the rest of her life wouldn't be
found by floating endlessly in the Bahamas.

Time to get off the boat, Rena, she told herself with a sudden smile. The next adventure's always just around the corner. Not knowing what it would be only made the search more intriguing.

The first long, loud blast of the horn was her signal. Drawing back from the rail, Serena went to her cabin to change.

Within thirty minutes she entered the ship's casino dressed in the modified tux that was her uniform. She had pulled her hair back in a loose bun at the nape of her neck so that it wouldn't tend to fall over her face. Her hands would soon be too busy to fool with it.

The chandeliers were lit, spilling light onto the red and gold art deco carpet. Long curved windows allowed a view of the glassed-in Promenade deck, then the blue-green stretch of sea. The remaining walls were lined with slot machines, as silent as soldiers waiting for an attack. Fussing with the bow tie she could never seem to get quite right, Serena crossed to her supervisor. As with any sailor, the shifting of the ship under her feet went unnoticed.

"Serena MacGregor reporting for duty, sir," she said crisply.

Turning, a clipboard in one hand, he looked her up and down. Dale Zimmerman's lightweight boxer's build skimmed just under six feet. He had a smooth, handsome face he dedicatedly tanned, winning crinkles at the corners of his light blue eyes, and sun-bleached hair that curled riotously. He had a reputation, which he assiduously promoted, of being a marvelous lover. After his brief study of Serena, his grin broke out.

"Rena, can't you ever get this thing right?" Tucking the clipboard under his arm, Dale straightened her tie.

"I like to give you something to do."

"You know, lover, if you're serious about quitting after this run, this is going to be your last chance for paradise." Tugging on her tie, he lifted his eyes to grin into hers.

Serena cocked a brow. What had begun a year ago as an ardent pursual on Dale's part had been tempered into a good-humored joke about Serena's refusal to go to bed with him. They had become, more to his surprise than hers, friends. "I'm going to hate to miss it," Serena told him with a sigh. "Did the little redhead from South Dakota go home happy?" she asked with a guileless smile.

Dale's eyes narrowed. "Anybody ever tell you that you see too much?"

"All the time. What's my table?"

"You're on two." Taking out a cigarette, Dale lit it as she walked away. If anyone had told him a year before that a classy number like Serena MacGregor would not only hold him off but make him feel fraternal, he'd have recommended a good psychiatrist. With a shrug he went back to his clipboard. He was going to regret losing her, Dale reflected, and not only because of his personal feelings. She was the best damn blackjack dealer he had.

There were eight blackjack tables scattered throughout the casino. Serena and the seven other dealers would rotate from position to position through the rest of the afternoon and evening, with only a brief, staggered dinner break. Unless the playing was light, the casino would stay open until two. If it was heavy, a few tables might stay open until three. The first rule was to give the passengers what they wanted.

Other men and women clad in tuxedos went to their stations. Beside Serena the young Italian who had just been promoted to croupier stood at table two. Serena gave him a smile, remembering that Dale had asked her to keep an eye on him.

"Enjoy yourself, Tony," she suggested, eyeing the crowd that already waited outside the glass doors. "It's going to be a long night." And all on our feet, she added silently as Dale gave the signal to open the door.

Passengers poured in. Not in a trickle--they rarely trickled in the first day of a cruise. The crowd would thin during the dinner hours, then swell again until past midnight. Dress was casual—shorts, jeans, bare feet—the uniform for afternoon gambling. With the opening of the door Serena heard the musical sound effects of arcade games already being fed on the Promenade deck. Within minutes the sound was drowned out by the steady clatter of slots.

Serena could separate the gamblers from the "players" and the players from the "lookers." There was always some of each group in any batch of passengers. There would be a percentage who had never been in a casino before. They would simply wander around, attracted by the noise and the colorful equipment before they exchanged their bills for change for the slots.

There were some who came for fun, not really caring if they won or lost. These were the players—they came for the game. It usually took little time for the looker to become the player. They would shout when they won and moan when they lost in much the same way the arcade addicts reacted.

But always, there were the gamblers. They would haunt the casino during the trip, turning the game of win and lose into an art—or an obsession. They had no specific features, no particular mode of dress. The mystique of the riverboat gambler could be found in the neat little grandmother from Peoria just as it could be found in the Madison Avenue executive. As the tables began to fill, Serena categorized them. She smiled at the five people who had chosen her table, then broke the seal on four decks of cards.

"Welcome aboard," she said, and began to shuffle.

It took only an hour for the scent of gambling to rise. It permeated the smoke and light sweat that drifted through the casino. It was a heady scent, tempting. Serena had always wondered if it was what drew people more than the lights and green baize. The scent, and the noise of silver clattering in the bowls of the slot machines. Serena never played them, perhaps because she recognized the gambler in herself. She'd decided long ago not to risk anything unless the odds were on her side.

During her first shift she changed tables every thirty minutes, making her way slowly around the room. After her dinner break it began again. The casino grew more crowded after the sun set. Tables were full and the roulette wheel spun continuously. Dress became more elegant, as if to gamble in the evening required glamor.

Because the cards and people always changed, Serena was never bored. She had chosen the job to meet people—not the cut-out-of-the-same-affluent-cloth people she'd met in college, but a variety. In that she'd accomplished her goal. At the moment she had a Texan, two New Yorkers, a Korean and a Georgian at her table, all of whom she'd identified by their accents. This was as much a part of the game for her as the cards she slid onto the baize. One she never tired of.

Serena dealt the second card around, peeked at her hole card, and was satisfied with an eighteen. The first New Yorker took a hit, counted his cards, and gave a disgusted grunt. With a shake of the head he indicated that he'd stand. The Korean busted on twenty-two, then rose from the table with a mutter. The second New Yorker, a sleek blonde in a narrow black dinner dress, held with a nine and a queen.

"I'll take one," the man from Georgia drawled. He counted eighteen, gave Serena a thoughtful look, and held.

The man from Texas took his time. He had fourteen and didn't like the eight Serena had showing. Considering the possibilities, he stroked his chin, swilled some bourbon, then motioned Serena to hit him. She did, a tad too hard with a nine.

"Sweetheart," he said as he leaned on the table, "you're just too pretty to take a man's money that way."

"Sorry." With a smile she turned over her hole card. "Eighteen," she announced before she settled the betting.

Serena saw the hundred-dollar bill on the table

before she realized someone had taken the Korean's
vacant stool. Glancing up, she met a pair of green
eyes—cool, depthless, direct. She stared, trapped in
that instant of contact into seeing nothing else. Cool
green, with amber rimming the iris. Something like ice
skidded down her spine. Forcing herself to blink,
Serena looked at the man.

He had the lean face of an aristocrat, but this was no
prince. Serena sensed it instantly. Perhaps it was the
long, unsmiling mouth, or the rough sweep of black
brows. Or perhaps it was simply the inner warning that
went off in her brain. A ruler yes, but not royalty. This
was the type of man who planned ruthless coups and
succeeded. His hair flowed over his ears thick and black
and down to the collar of a white silk shirt. The skin
stretched taut over the long bones of his face was as
tanned as Dale's, but Serena didn't think he worked on
the tone like her supervisor. This man faced the
elements without a thought for fashion.

He didn't slouch like the Texan or lounge indolently
like the man from Georgia, but rather sat like a sleek,
patient cat, always coiled to spring. It wasn't until one
rough brow rose slightly in question that Serena realized she'd been staring.

"Change a hundred," she said briskly, annoyed with
herself. With deft movements she slipped the bill into
the slot of the table, then counted out chips. When the
bets were placed, she dealt the cards.

The man from New York glanced at the ten Serena
had showing and hit on fourteen. He broke. The new
player held on fifteen with a wordless gesture of his
hand. She broke the other New Yorker and the Geor-

gian before the Texan held on nineteen. Serena turned over a three to go with her ten, dealt herself a deuce, then broke with twenty-three. The man with the dangerous face drew out a thin cigar and continued to play silently. Serena already knew he was a gambler.

His name was Justin Blade. His ancestors had ridden swift ponies and hunted with bow and arrow. Serena had been right about the aristocracy, though his bloodline wasn't royal. Part of his heritage came from simple French immigrants and a dash from Welsh miners. The rest was Comanche.

He hadn't known a reservation, and though he had brushed with poverty in his youth, he was well accustomed to the feel of silk against his skin. Accustomed enough so that like the very wealthy, he rarely noticed it. His first stake had been won in the backroom of a pool hall when he'd been fifteen. In the twenty years since, he'd played more elegant games. He was, as Serena had sensed, a gambler. And he was already figuring the odds.

Justin had entered the casino with the notion of passing a few hours with a mild game. A man could relax with small stakes when he could afford to lose. Then he'd seen her. His eyes had passed over other women in sleek dinner dress, the gleam of gold and sparkle of jewels, and came to rest on the blonde in the mannish tuxedo. She had a slender neck which her hairstyle and the ruffled shirtfront accentuated, and a carriage that shouted breeding. But what was more, what he had sensed in the loins, was a blatant sexuality that required no movement, no words on her part. She was a woman a man would beg for.

Justin watched her hands as she dealt. They were exquisite—narrow, long-fingered, with delicate blue veins just under the surface of creamy skin. Her nails were oval and perfect, with the gleam of clear polish. They were hands suited to fragile teacups and French pastries. The kind of hands a man burned to have on his skin.

Lifting his eyes from them, Justin looked directly into hers. With the faintest of frowns Serena stared back. Why was it, she wondered, that this dark, silent man brought her both discomfort and curiosity? He hadn't spoken a word since he'd sat down—not to her nor to any of the others at her table. Though he'd been winning with professional consistency, he didn't appear to gain any pleasure from it. He didn't appear to be paying attention to the game if it came to that, she told herself. All he did was stare at her with that same calm, watchful expression.

"Fifteen," Serena said coolly, indicating the cards in front of him. Justin nodded for the hit and took a six without the slightest change of expression.

"Damn if you don't have the luck, son," the Texan stated jovially. Glancing at his own meager pile of chips, he gave a quick grimace. "Glad somebody does." He wheezed as Serena dealt him the card that eased him out at twenty-two.

Turning over twenty for the house, she collected chips, then slid two twenty-five-dollar markers to Justin. His fingertips covered hers over them. The touch was light, but potent enough to have her eyes flashing up to his. Watching her steadily, he made no move to take his hand from hers. There was no pressure, no flirtatious squeeze, but Serena felt the response shoot through her as though their bodies rather than their fingers had pressed together. Calling on all her control, she slowly brought her hand back to her side.

"New dealer," she said calmly, noting with relief that her shift at that station was finished. "Have a nice evening." She moved to the next station, swearing to herself she wouldn't look back. Of course she did, and found her eyes pinned to his.

Infuriated, she allowed herself a slight toss of her head. Her expression became challenging. For the first time that evening she saw the long mouth curve in a slow smile—a smile that barely shifted the angles and planes on his face. Justin inclined his head, as if accepting the challenge. Serena turned her back on him.

"Good evening," she said in a clear voice to the new set of players.

The moon was still high, cutting a swath of light across the black water. From the rail Serena could see the white tips of waves as the ship moved in a fast sea. It was after two A.M., and the deck was deserted. She liked this time of the morning, while the passengers slept, before the crew began its early shift. She was alone with the sea and the wind and could imagine herself in any era she chose.

She breathed deeply, inhaling the scent of salt spray and night. They'd be in Nassau just past dawn, and while in port the casino would be closed. She would have the morning free to do as she chose. She preferred the night.

Her mind drifted back to her working hours, to the silent gambler who'd sat at her table, winning and watching. She thought he was a man women would be drawn to but wasn't surprised that he'd been alone. A solitary man, Serena mused, and strangely compelling. Attractive, she admitted as she leaned farther out to let the wind whip at her face. Attractive in a dangerous sort of way. But then, it was in her blood to look on danger as a challenge. Risks could be calculated, percentages measured, and yet . . . And yet Serena didn't think the man would follow the neat path of theory.

"Night suits you."

Serena's hands tightened on the rail. Though she'd never heard him speak, though she hadn't even heard his approach, she knew who stood behind her. It took all her effort not to gasp and whirl. While her heart hammered she turned to watch him come out of the shadows. Wanting her voice to be steady, she gave herself a moment while he stopped to stand beside her at the rail.

"Did your luck hold?" she asked.

Justin kept his eyes on her face. "Apparently."

She tried, and failed, to place his origin through his accent. His voice was deep and smooth and without inflection. "You're very good," she stated. "We don't often get a professional in the casino." There seemed to be a quick flash of humor in his eyes before he drew out a slim cigar and lit it. Smoke stung the air, then vanished in the wind. Serena relaxed her fingers on the rail, one at a time. "Are you enjoying your trip?"

"More than I anticipated." He took a slow, thoughtful drag on the cigar. "Are you?"

Serena smiled. "It's my job."

Justin leaned back against the rail, resting his hand beside hers. "That's not an answer, Serena," he pointed out.

Since there was a name tag on her lapel, she only lifted a brow at his use of her name. "I enjoy it, Mr.—"

"Blade," he said softly as he ran a fingertip down her jawline. "Justin Blade. Remember it."

Serena refused to back up though the lightning response of her body to his touch surprised her. Instead, she regarded him steadily. "I've a good memory."

With a trace of a smile he nodded. "Yes, that's why you're a good dealer. How long have you been doing it?"

"A year." Though he removed his fingertip, her blood didn't cool.

Surprised, Justin took a last drag on his cigar, then crushed it under his foot. "I would have thought longer from the way you handle the cards." Taking her hand from the rail, he studied the back, then turned it over to look at the palm. Soft, he thought, and steady. An interesting combination. "What did you do before?"

Even as her brain told her retreat would be wise, Serena allowed her hand to remain in his. She sensed strength and skill in the touch, though she wasn't certain of the aspect of either. "I studied."

"What?"

"Whatever interested me. What do you do?"

"Whatever interests me."

She laughed, a low sultry sound that whispered along his skin. "Somehow I think you mean that quite literally, Mr. Blade." She started to remove her hand, but his fingers closed over it.

"I do," he murmured. "It's Justin, Serena." His eyes skimmed the deserted deck, then the dark, endless sea. "This isn't the place for formality."

Common sense told her to tread carefully; instinct drove her to provoke. "There are rules for the crew when dealing with passengers, Mr. Blade," she said coolly. "I need my hand."

When he smiled, the moonlight glittered in his eyes, like a cat's. "So do I." Lifting it, he pressed his lips deep in the center of her palm. Serena felt the aftershock of the kiss in every pore. "I take what I need," he murmured against her flesh.

Her breathing had quickened without her being aware of it. On the dark, empty deck he was barely more than a shadow with a voice that might have been pressed through honey, and dangerous eyes. Feeling her body yearning toward him, Serena restrained it with a quick flash of temper.

"Not this time. I'm going in, it's late."

Keeping her hand firmly in his, Justin reached up to pull the pins from her hair. As it tumbled over her shoulders, he tossed them into the sea. Stunned by his audacity, Serena glared at him. "Late," he agreed, combing his fingers from the crown to the tips of the thick, blond mane. "But you're a woman for the dark hours. I thought so the moment I saw you." With a movement that was too quick and too smooth to be measured, he had Serena trapped between his body and the rail. Her hair flew toward the sea, pulled by the wind, her skin pure as marble in the moonlight. Justin discovered the need was stronger than he had realized.

"Do you know what I thought?" Serena demanded, struggling to keep her words from jerking. "I thought you were rude and annoying."

He laughed, a rich quick sound of amusement. "It seems we were both right. Should I tell you it very nearly distracted me from my game, wondering how you tasted?"

Serena became very still. The only movement came from the rich strands of gold that danced around her face. Then her chin rose; her eyes darkened with challenge. "A pity," she said quietly as she curled her hand into a fist. Passenger or no passenger, she determined, she was going to give him a good swift punch, just the way her brothers had taught her.

"It's rare for anything or anyone to interfere with my concentration." As he spoke he leaned closer. Serena tensed her muscles. "You have the eyes of a witch. I'm a superstitious man."

"Arrogant," Serena corrected steadily. "But I doubt superstitious."

She saw the smile in his eyes only as his face dominated her vision. "Don't you believe in luck, Serena?"

"Yes." And a good right jab, she added silently. She felt his fingers slide beneath her blowing hair to cup the base of her neck. His mouth lowered toward hers. Somehow the warm flutter of his breath caused her lips to part and her concentration to waver.

One hand still held hers, and he circled the palm with a finger as if to remind her of the feel of his lips on her flesh. Fighting the growing weakness, Serena drew back, aiming for his vulnerable, unsuspecting stomach.

Less than an inch away from target, her fist was captured in a hard grip. Frustrated, she struggled, only to hear his quiet laugh again. "Your eyes give you away," he told her, holding her still. "You'll have to work on it."

"If you don't let me go, I'll . . ." The threat trailed off as his lips brushed hers. It wasn't a kiss, but a temptation. Her tongue came out to moisten her lips as if in anticipation of something darkly sweet and strictly forbidden.

"What?" he whispered, touching his mouth to hers again with a lightness that had the blood pounding in his head. He wanted to crush and devour almost as much as he wanted to savor. Her lips were damp and she smelled faintly of the sea and summer. When she didn't answer, Justin traced the shape of her mouth with his tongue, committing it to memory while he absorbed the flavor and waited.

Serena felt the thick, liquefying pleasure seep into her. Her lids were too heavy and fluttered closed; her muscles relaxed. The fist still curled in his hand went limp. For the first time in her memory her mind went blank—a clean slate on which he could have written anything he desired. She felt the tiny arousing pain as he nipped into her full bottom lip, and her mind filled again. But not with thoughts.

His body was against hers, hard and lean. His mouth was so soft, softer than she thought any man's could be, like the brush of fine silk against naked flesh. There was the faint scent of tobacco, something rich and foreign, and the smell of him without the interference of cologne. He whispered her name as she had never heard it spoken before. The boat listed, but he swayed with it as easily as she as he gathered her closer. With no more thoughts of resisting, Serena let her arms curve around his neck, her head dropping back in invitation.

Justin felt an almost savage need to plunder as he gripped her hair in his hand. "Open your eyes," he demanded. While he watched, the heavy lids opened to reveal eyes misted with pleasure. "Look at me when I kiss you," he murmured.

Then his mouth crushed hers, ruthless, ravaging. He could hear his own heartbeat raging in his chest as he plunged deeper. He discovered tastes, endless flavors, in the recesses he explored as her tongue answered with equal urgency. His eyes were only slits while he watched the misty pleasure in hers smolder into passion then become opaque. On a moan they closed, and his own vision blurred.

Serena felt desire grip her as if it had claws. Wants, needs, secrets, were exposed in one tumultuous explosion. Even as she hungered to fulfill them she realized he was a man who could strip her to the soul. And she knew nothing of him. Frightened, she struggled to free herself, but he held her close, his lips clinging until he was done. In some sane portion of her brain she realized he would always take without regard for willingness.

When she was free, Serena took time to catch her

breath. Justin watched her again with that strange ability he had for absolute stillness and absolute silence. There would be no reading his eyes. In a habitual defense Serena turned her fear into anger.

"If you read your brochure, you'll see that your passage fee doesn't include your pick of the crew."

"Certain things have no price, Serena."

Something in his tone made her tremble. It was as if he'd already put his mark on her, a mark she wouldn't easily erase. She backed into the shadows. "Stay away from me," she warned him.

Justin leaned back on the rail, keeping his gaze on her silhouette. "No," he said mildly. "I've already dealt the cards, and the odds always favor the house."

"Well, I'm not interested," she hissed. "So deal me out." Turning, she clattered down the stairs that led to the next deck.

Slipping his hands into his pockets, Justin jingled change and smiled. "Not a chance."

Chapter Two

Serena slipped into a pair of khaki shorts, then crawled under her bunk to find her sandals. According to her calculations, most of the passengers who would disembark for their day on Nassau would have already done so. There was little chance of being caught in the crush or of having to weave her way through the waiting cab drivers and tour guides on the docks. Since it would be her last trip there, Serena wanted to play tourist herself and pick up a few souvenirs to take home to her family. Cursing the sandal which had somehow tucked itself into a far corner, she squiggled farther under the bunk.

"You'd think I'd learn to be neat after living in a closet for a year," she muttered, wiggling back out again.

If she lay full length, she could touch each side wall

of the cabin. In the other direction she had about two feet to spare. Beside the bunk there was a tiny mirrored dresser bolted to the floor and a cubbyhole that passed for closet space. She'd often thought it was a lucky thing she didn't suffer from claustrophobia.

Still on the floor, she pushed the sandals on her feet, then began to check the contents of the tote bag she would carry. A wallet and sunglasses. Well, she couldn't think of anything else that was necessary, Serena reflected as she jumped lightly to her feet. Briefly she considered asking one of the other dealers if they wanted to join her, then rejected the idea. She wasn't in the best of moods, and it wouldn't take anyone who'd worked closely with her long to notice it, and perhaps ferret out the reason.

The last thing Serena wanted to discuss was Justin Blade. In fact, she added smartly as she pulled a khaki tennis cap over her hair, the last thing she wanted to even *think* about was Justin Blade with his cool green eyes, long, unsmiling mouth, and ruthless good looks.

When Serena realized she *was* thinking about him, she left her cabin in an even poorer mood. Only nine more days, she reminded herself as she ignored the elevator and marched up the steps. She could put up with anything for nine days.

With a smirk Serena remembered the salesman from Detroit who had haunted her table throughout a cruise the previous spring. He'd gone so far as to follow her down to the crew's quarters and try to talk his way into her cabin. She'd dispatched him by claiming her lover was the chief engineer, a swarthy Italian with biceps like cinder blocks. Serena's smirk faded. Somehow she didn't think that tactic would work with a man like Justin Blade.

As she climbed upward, the threadbare carpet of the crew's decks was replaced by the bold red and gold pattern that graced the rest of the ship. Ornate light fixtures lit the landings rather than the plain glass shields of belowdecks. Coming out on the main level, she exchanged a quick word of greeting with other members of the crew still on board.

Two men lounged on either side of the gangway— one in the crisp white uniform of the first mate, the other in casual cruise wear. As usual, they were arguing intensely but without heat. Serena caught the eye of the cruise director first, a small Englishman with sandy hair and boundless energy. She winked at him, then planted herself in between the two men.

"What diplomat put the two of you on gangway duty together?" she asked with a mock sigh. "I suppose I'll have to play referee again. What is it this time?"

"Rob claims that Mrs. Dewalter is a rich widow," Jack, the Englishman, began in his rounded tones. "I say she's divorced."

"A widow," the first mate stated again, folding his arms. "A beautiful rich widow."

"Mrs. Dewalter," Serena mused.

"Tall," Jack began. "Short, sculptured red hair."

"Built," Rob added.

"Philistine," Jack put in mildly, then addressed himself to Serena. "A rather gamine face."

"Okay," Serena said slowly, getting the picture of a woman she'd seen briefly in the casino the night before. "Widowed or divorced?" she inquired, well used to the picky arguments between the two men. "What about rings?"

"Exactly." Rob pounced on the question with a smirk for his associate. "She wore rings. Widows wear rings."

"So do bubble-brained first mates," Jack pointed out with a glance at the signet ring on Rob's hand.

"The point is," Serena interrupted before Rob could retort. "What sort of rings? A gold band? A jeweled circlet?"

"A chunk of ice as big as a hen's egg," Rob told her, giving Jack another satisfied sneer. "Rich widow."

"Divorced," Serena disagreed, bursting his bubble. "Sorry, if we go with the percentages, Rob, that's the most likely answer. Hen's eggs are rarely worn for sentimental value." After patting his cheek in consolation, she gave him a snappy salute. "Permission to go ashore, sir!"

"Get out of here." He gave her a quick nudge. "Go buy a straw mat."

"My plans exactly." With a laugh, she jogged down the narrow iron steps to the dock.

The sun was brilliant, the air moist and balmy. Serena bargained with a few boys who loitered on the docks hawking shell necklaces and decided it wouldn't be such a bad day after all. She had hours before her to do as she chose in one of the prettiest tourist spots in the Bahamas.

"Three dollars," the lean-limbed black boy told her, holding out handfuls of dark-shelled necklaces. He wore only a pair of shorts and a medallion that was slowly oxidizing. His partner held a small portable radio to his ear, moving lithely to the scratchy reggae beat.

"You pirate," Serena said good-naturedly. "One dollar."

The boy grinned, sensing a true haggler. "Oh, pretty lady," he began in his high, sing-song voice. "If I could, I would give you the necklace for only your smile, but then my father would beat me."

Serena lifted a brow. "Yes, I can see how abused you are. One dollar and a quarter."

"Two-fifty. I gathered the shells myself and strung them by the light of a candle."

With a laugh Serena shook her head. "The next thing you'll tell me is you fought off a school of sharks."

"No sharks near our island, my lady," he said proudly. "Two American dollars."

"One and a half American dollars because I admire your imagination." Digging into her tote, she drew out her wallet. The money was out of her hands and into the pocket of his shorts in the blink of an eye.

"For you, pretty lady, I will risk a beating."

Serena chose her necklace, then found herself giving him another quarter. "Pirate," she murmured as he grinned at her. Slinging her tote over her shoulder, she started to walk away.

It was then that she saw him, standing alone on the dock behind her. Serena wasn't as surprised as she thought she should've been. But then somehow she'd known she'd see him. He wore a plain beige T-shirt that made his skin seem nearly copper, and a faded pair of cutoffs that accentuated his lean, muscular thighs and rangy build. Though the sun was glaring fiercely, he wore no tinted glasses or other protection. He didn't seem to need it. Just as she was debating whether she should simply walk by him, he came toward her. He moved lightly, with the grace of a hunter—a man, she thought for no specific reason, who was more accustomed to sand or grass than asphalt.

"Good morning." Justin took her hand as though the meeting had been arranged.

"Good morning," she returned frostily, refusing to give him any satisfaction by tugging on her hand. "Didn't you sign up for any of the tours?"

"No. I don't care to be directed." He began to walk toward town with Serena in tow.

Biting back words of fury, she spoke in a calculatedly pleasant voice. "Several of the tours are very worthwhile. They're really the best way to see the island in the limited amount of time we're in port."

"You've been here before," he said easily. "Why don't you show me?"

"I'm off duty," Serena stated crisply. "And I'm going shopping."

"Fine. Since you've already begun," he said, glancing down at the necklace she still held in her hand, "where do you want to go next?"

She decided to give up diplomacy altogether. "Will you please go away? I plan to enjoy myself today."

"So do I."

"Alone," she said pointedly.

Stopping, he turned to her. "Ever hear about Americans sticking together on foreign soil?" he asked as he took the necklace from her fingers and slipped it over her head.

"No," she returned, wishing she didn't want so badly to smile.

"I'll explain it to you while we take a carriage ride."

"I'm going shopping," she reminded him as he led her toward town.

"You'll have a better idea where to buy what after a ride."

"Justin." Serena matched his stride because it was better than being hauled. "Do you ever take no for an answer?"

He appeared to think this over before he shook his head. "Not that I remember."

"I didn't think so," she muttered, then stood eyeing him stonily.

"All right, let's try it this way. Heads, we go for a ride, tails you go shopping." Reaching into his pocket, he drew out a coin.

"Probably has two heads." Serena frowned suspiciously at the quarter.

"I never cheat," Justin said solemnly as he held the coin between his forefinger and thumb for her inspection.

She could refuse and simply walk away, Serena considered, but she found herself nodding. The odds were even. With a practiced flick of the wrist, Justin sent the coin spinning in the air, nabbed it, then flipped it over on the back of his hand. Heads. Somehow she'd known it would be.

"Never bet against the house," Serena mumbled as she climbed into a carriage.

As the horse began its meandering clip-clop down the street, Serena thought about maintaining a dignified silence—for about thirty seconds. Knowing herself well, she was forced to admit that if she hadn't wanted to get into the carriage, she wouldn't have gotten into it. Not without a fuss. So instead of a dignified silence, Serena dropped her tote bag on the floor of the carriage, ignored the charm of the narrow little street, and stared at her companion.

"What are you doing here?"

He tossed an arm over the seat, his fingers skimming over her hair. "Enjoying the ride."

"No smart answers, Justin. You wanted my company and you've got it unless I decide to scream assault and jump out of the carriage."

He eyed her a moment, first in curiosity, then in admiration. She'd do just that. He dropped his fingers to the nape of her neck. "What do you want to know?"

"What are you doing on the *Celebration?*" Serena demanded, shifting away from the pleasure his fingers brought her. "You don't strike me as the type of man who'd go on a relaxing tropical cruise."

"A friend recommended it. I was restless, he was persuasive." His fingers brushed her neck again. "What are you doing on the *Celebration?*"

"Dealing blackjack."

His brow rose at her answer. "Why?"

"I was restless." In spite of herself, Serena smiled.

The driver started to begin his monologue on the highlights of the island, but noted that the couple wasn't interested in anything but each other. He clicked his tongue at his horse, then remained silent.

"All right, where are you from?" Serena asked,

looking for a starting point. "I have a habit of placing people in regions, and I can't place you."

Justin smiled enigmatically. "I travel."

"Originally," she persisted, narrowing her eyes at the evasion.

"Nevada."

"Vegas." Serena nodded. "You've spent some time there. I imagine it's a good town for people with the right skills." When he only shrugged, Serena studied his profile. "And that's how you make your living? Gambling?"

Justin turned his head until his eyes met hers. "Yes. Why?"

"There were only two gamblers at that table last night," Serena mused. "You and the man from Georgia, though he was a milder sort."

"And the others?" Justin asked, his curiosity piqued.

"Oh, the Texan just likes a game; he doesn't put that much thought into it. The blonde from New York thinks she's a gambler." Because the gentle swaying of the carriage was soothing, Serena smiled a little and relaxed. "But she can't keep up with the cards or the odds. She'll end up dropping a bundle or winning on sheer luck. The other man from New York watches the cards but doesn't know how to bet. You have the concentration that separates a gambler from a player."

"A very interesting theory," Justin reflected. With a fingertip he slid Serena's sunglasses down the bridge of her nose so he could see her eyes without interference. "Do you play, Serena?"

"Depends on the game and the odds," she told him,

pushing the glasses back up. "I don't like to lose." From the look in his eyes she realized they hadn't been speaking of cards, but a more dangerous game.

Smiling, he leaned back again, gesturing toward the right with his hand. "They have beautiful beaches here."

"Hmmm."

As if on cue, the driver began his spiel again, giving a running commentary on the island until he brought them back to their starting point.

The streets were filled with people now, the majority of them tourists with bulging shopping bags and cameras. Both sides of the road were lined with little shops, some with their doors open, all with their windows crowded with displays. "Well, thanks for the ride." Serena started to climb down, but Justin circled her waist with his hands and lifted her lightly.

He held her an inch above the ground for a moment while she gripped his shoulders for balance. Her lightness surprised him, making him realize that her sexuality and style had blinded him to how small she was. His fingers became abruptly gentle as he set her on the ground.

"Thanks," Serena managed after she'd cleared her throat. "Enjoy your day."

"I intend to," he told her as he took her hand again.

"Justin . . ." Serena took a deep breath. The time had come, she decided, to take a firm stand. That brief instant when he had held her had reminded her how foolish she had been to relax even for a moment. "I took your carriage ride, now I'm going shopping."

"Fine. I'll go with you."

"I'm looking for souvenirs, Justin," she said discouragingly. "You know, T-shirts, straw boxes. You'll be bored."

"I'm never bored."

"You will be this time," she told him as he began to meander down the street, his fingers laced with hers. "I promise."

"How about an ashtray that says Welcome to Nassau?" Justin suggested blandly.

Valiantly she swallowed a chuckle. "I'm going in here," Serena stated, stopping on impulse at the first shop they came to. And, she determined, she would stop at every shop on Bay Street until she successfully drove him crazy.

By the time her tote bag contained musical key chains, assorted T-shirts, and shell boxes, Serena had forgotten she had wanted to be rid of him. He made her laugh—the gentlest seduction. For a man she had instinctively termed a loner, Justin was easy company. Before long Serena had not only stopped being resentful, she'd stopped being wary.

"Oh, look!" She grabbed a coconut shell that had been fashioned into a grinning head.

"Elegant," Justin stated, turning it over in his hands.

"It's ridiculous, you fool." Laughing, Serena fished out her wallet. "And perfect for my brother. Caine's ridiculous too. . . . Well, not all the time," she added scrupulously.

The aisles of the straw market were crammed with people and merchandise, but not so crowded that

Serena couldn't worm her way through in search of treasures. Spotting a large woven bag overhead, she pointed. Justin obligingly lifted it down to her.

"It's nearly as big as you are," he decided as she took it from him.

"It's not for me," Serena murmured, studying it minutely. "My mother does a lot of needlework; this should be handy for carting it around with her."

"Handmade." Serena glanced down at the large dark-skinned woman in a rocking chair, smoking a little brown pipe. "Myself," she added, patting her generous bosom. "Nothing made in Hong Kong in my stall."

"You do beautiful work," Serena told her, though the woman already interested her more than the bag.

Lifting a large palm fan, the islander nodded majestically and began to stir the sultry air. Serena was fascinated to see a ring on every thick finger. "You buy something pretty for your lady today?" she asked Justin with a flash of white teeth.

"No, not yet," Justin said before Serena could speak. "What do you suggest?"

"Justin—"

"Here." The old woman cut Serena off, turning to push back some cloth at her right. With a few wheezes and grunts she pulled out a cream-colored dashiki-style tunic with a border of bold rainbow stitches. "Special," the woman told Justin, pushing it into his hands. "Lots of purple here, like your lady's eyes."

"Blue," Serena began, "and I'm not—"

"Let's see." Justin held it up in front of her, surveying the effect through narrowed eyes. "Yes, it suits you," he decided.

"You wear it for your man tonight," the woman advised, already folding it into a bag. "Very sexy."

"An excellent idea," Justin agreed as he started to count out bills.

"Wait a minute." Serena pointed at him with the hand that still held the straw bag. "He is not my man."

"Not your man?" The woman went into peals of laughter, rocking back and forth in the chair until it screeched in protest. "Honey, this your man for sure, you can't trick a seventh daughter of a seventh daughter. No indeed. You want the bag too?"

"Well, I . . ." Serena stared down at the straw bag as if she hadn't a clue how it had gotten into her hand.

"The bag too." Justin peeled off more bills. "Thank you."

The money disappeared into her huge hand as she continued to rock. "You enjoy our island."

"Now, wait—"

But Justin was already pulling her along. "You can't argue with a seventh daughter of a seventh daughter, Serena. You never know what curse she'll toss at you."

"Nonsense," she stated, but glanced cautiously over her shoulder to where the big woman sat rocking. "And you can't buy me clothes, Justin. I don't even know you."

"I already did."

"Well, you shouldn't have. And you paid for my mother's bag."

"My compliments to your mother."

She sighed, squinting as they emerged into daylight. "You're a very difficult man."

"There, you see? You do know me." Taking her

sunglasses from the top of her hat, he slid them back in front of her eyes. "Hungry?"

"Yes." The corners of her mouth twitched, so Serena gave up and smiled. "Yes, I am."

With his eyes on hers he slowly circled her palm with a fingertip. "How about a picnic on the beach?"

It wasn't a simple matter to ignore the tingling that was now racing up her arm, but she managed a casual shrug. "If you had food, and if you had transportation, and if you had some cold island concoction to drink, I might be interested."

"Anything else?" Justin asked as he stopped to lean on the hood of a Mercedes.

"Not that I can think of."

"Okay, let's go then." Pulling keys out of his pocket, Justin walked around to unlock the passenger door of the car.

With her tote bag dangling from her fingers, Serena stared. "Do you mean this is your car?"

"No, this is the car I rented. There's a cooler in the trunk. Do you like cold chicken?"

When he tossed the bags into the backseat, Serena put her hands on her hips. "You were awfully damn sure of yourself, weren't you?"

"Just playing the odds," he claimed, then cupped her chin in his hand and brushed her lips with his. "Just playing the odds."

Serena dropped into the passenger seat not certain if she admired or detested his sheer nerve. "I'd like to know what cards he has up his sleeve," she muttered as he rounded the hood to join her.

She noticed Justin drove as he did everything else,

with the arrogant ease of control. He seemed acclimated to driving on the left side of the road as if he did so daily.

They passed under the fat leaves of almond trees, beside thick green grapes which would be purple in another month. Branches laden with the bright orange blossoms typical of the island danced in the breeze as they drew nearer to the sea. He didn't speak, and again she noticed he had that oddly admirable capacity for silence. Yet it wasn't soothing, but exciting.

It occurred to her as they drove by the graceful colonial homes of the wealthy toward the public beaches that true relaxation was something not often experienced around a man like Justin Blade. Then the thought came quickly—too quickly—that relaxation was something she rarely looked for.

Turning in her seat, Serena exchanged the tropical beauty of Nassau for Justin's handsome, almost hawkish features. A gambler, she mused. A shipboard acquaintance. Serena had too much experience with the two to trust in any deep, lasting relationship. Still, she thought that if she were careful, she might enjoy his companionship for a few days.

What harm could there be in getting to know him a bit better? In spending some of her free time with him? She wasn't like some of her coworkers in the casino who fell in and out of love with each other or lost their hearts to a passenger only to be miserable and desolated at the end of a cruise. When a woman had managed to keep her heart in one piece for twenty-six years, she wasn't about to lose it in ten days . . . was she?

Justin turned to give her one of his cool, unsmiling looks. Butterflies fluttered in her throat. She'd be very careful, Serena decided, as if she were walking through a minefield.

"What are you thinking?"

"About bombs," she answered blandly. "Deadly, camouflaged bombs." She gave him a quick, innocent grin. "Are we going to eat soon? I'm starving."

With a last brief look, Justin pulled off to the side of the road. "How's this?"

Serena gazed out over the white sand to the intense blue of the ocean. "Perfect." Stepping from the car, she took a deep breath of blossoms and sea and hot sand. "I don't do this often. When the ship's in port I usually catch up on my sleep or my reading, or give another shot at getting a tan on deck. I've lost count of the number of times I've been docked at this island."

"Didn't you take the job on the ship to travel?" He took a small cooler and a folded blanket from the trunk.

"No, it was the people really. I wanted to find out just how many kinds of people there were in the world." Serena slipped off her sandals to feel the warm sand on her feet. "We have more than five hundred in the crew, and only ten Americans. You'd be amazed at the variety of people you meet. It's like a floating U.N." Taking the blanket from under his arm, Serena snapped it open, then let it billow onto the sand. "I've dealt cards to people from every continent." She seated herself Indian fashion on the edge of the blanket. "I'll miss that."

"Miss it?" Justin dropped down beside her. "Are you quitting?"

Tossing her hat aside, Serena shook back her hair. "It's time. I want to catch up with my family for a while before I do anything else."

"Anything else in mind?"

"I've been thinking about a hotel casino." She pursed her lips in thought. It was a project she intended to discuss with her father soon. He'd know the best way to go about financing property and a building.

"You've had the experience," Justin mused, believing she was considering applying for a job as a dealer. "The only difference would be you'd deal on dry land." An idea germinated in his mind, but he decided to wait before approaching her with it. "Where's your family?"

"Hmmm? Oh, Massachusetts." Her gaze fell on the cooler. "Feed me." When he opened the lid she noticed the napkins and cutlery came from the ship. "How'd you manage that?" Serena demanded. "The kitchen has a policy against making up picnic lunches."

"I bribed them," he said simply, and handed her a drumstick.

"Oh." She took a healthy bite. "Good thinking. What'd you get to drink?"

For an answer, Justin drew out a thermos and two plastic glasses with the ship's logo. "How's the chicken?"

"Terrific. Eat." She accepted the cup of dark pink liquid he handed her and sipped cautiously. It was richly fruity, smoothed with island rum. "Oh-oh, the *Celebrations* speciality." She gave the drink a dubious look. "I usually make it a policy not to get within a yard of one of these."

"You're on shore leave," Justin reminded her, plucking a piece of chicken from the cooler.

"And I want to live to tell about it," she murmured. For the moment she concentrated on the chicken and the pleasure of having no more to do than enjoy the breeze off the ocean.

"I would've thought the beaches would be more crowded," Justin commented.

"Mmm." Serena nodded as she drank again. "Most of the tourists who aren't shopping are on guided tours or scubaing on the other side of the island. It's off season too." She gestured with the drumstick before she dropped it onto a napkin. "The beaches aren't so quiet during the rush. But there's really a lot to see and do in Nassau besides swimming and sunbathing."

"Mmm." He watched her brush some sand from her thigh. "So our carriage driver said."

"I'm surprised you didn't ferry over to Paradise Island to the casinos for the day."

"Are you?" Leaning over, he took her hair in his hand. "It isn't the only game in town."

Justin touched his lips to hers, intending to give her a light, teasing kiss. But the intention evaporated at the warm, ripe taste. "How could I have forgotten how badly I want you?" he murmured, then drowned her muffled response with hard, unyielding pressure.

His tongue eased between lips he parted expertly as he pressed her back against the blanket. Feeling the muscled ridges of his body against hers, Serena started to object, but her arms were already around him, pulling him closer, her mouth was already searching, moving avidly under his.

The sun filtered through the leaves of the palm they lay under, flickering light over her closed lids until it was only a red mist dancing in front of her eyes. He kissed her as she'd never been kissed before, with lips and teeth and tongue, nibbling then devouring, seducing, then possessing. Mouth clung to mouth in a taste more potent than the rum they'd sampled.

A gull soared toward the sea with a long, wailing cry neither of them heard, then with a flick of a wing he was gone as if he'd never been. When Justin ran his hands down her arms, Serena felt his touch over every inch of her body. Her breasts ached from it; her thighs trembled. Longing for the imaginary to be real, she moaned and moved under him in invitation.

Ripping his mouth from hers, Justin pressed it against her throat as he struggled to cling to the fine edge of reason. He wanted her, wanted to feel her soft skin grow hot and moist under his hands. He wanted to touch every subtle curve and dip, feel every pulse hum and taste and taste until they were both raging.

Desire clawed at him with a sharpness he'd never experienced before as her hands moved over his back, pressing and kneading while he fought to remember they were not alone in a dark, quiet room. Had a woman ever taken him so far with only a kiss? He could only think of how much further she would take him when he was free to have all of her.

Nibbling and sucking, he ran his mouth up to her ear.

"Come back with me now, Serena." He licked the lobe before he caught it between his teeth. "Come back to my cabin with me. I want you."

His words seemed to float into her consciousness, almost drifting away before their meaning penetrated her passion. "No." Hearing her own weak protest, Serena fought to strengthen it. "No," she repeated, struggling away from him. Sitting up, she hugged her knees until her breathing leveled. "No," she said for a third time. "You have no right to—to—"

"To what?" Justin demanded, grabbing her face in his hands and jerking it back to him. "To want you or to show you that you want me?"

His eyes weren't cool now, but light and angry. Serena remembered her own first impression of ruthlessness and forced back a shudder before she pushed his hand away. "Don't tell me what I want," she tossed back. "If you're interested in a little shipboard fling, go find somebody else. You shouldn't have any trouble." Springing up, she strode furiously toward the sea. Justin caught her arm and spun her around.

"And don't you tell me what I'm interested in," he ordered curtly. "You didn't even know where we were. I could have taken you on a public beach in broad daylight."

"Really?" She threw her head back, infuriated that he spoke no less than the truth. "Well, if you're so sure of that, why didn't you?"

"Normally, I like my privacy, but keep pushing and I'll make an exception."

"And pigs fly," she said evenly as she turned toward the surf a second time. She'd no more than gotten her toes wet when he grabbed her again. For a moment Serena thought she had miscalculated. The rage in his eyes was nothing to tamper with, but she'd never had much luck controlling her temper once it had gotten beyond a certain point. When Justin dragged her against him, she cursed him.

He wanted to crush that hot, furious mouth again. Desire was raging through him as quickly as his temper, and one fed the other. Knowing what the outcome would be if he gave in to the first, Justin gave in to the second. Serena landed on her bottom in the shallows.

Shock covered her face first, then utter fury. "You— you *animal!*" Scrambling up, she launched herself at him, intent only on revenge. But when he grabbed her arms to ward her off, he was grinning.

"Would you believe you look beautiful when you're angry?"

The dip in the water hadn't cooled her temper. "You're going to pay for that one, Justin Blade." With her arms hampered she compensated with a kick but only ended up back in the water, tangled with him. "Get your hands off me, you jerk!" She shoved, submerged, and came up sputtering. "Nobody pushes a MacGregor around and gets away with it!"

In his attempt to prevent her from drowning both of them, his hand connected with her breast. The next moment he found that his mouth had covered hers again while his hand caressed through her wet, clinging shirt. Though he felt her moan of response, she continued to struggle, taking them both under again. He tasted salt, and her lips; he felt the slender thighs pressed against his as he rolled her over with the next

wave. With a muffled laugh he heard her swear at him
again as she gulped in air. Then the water tossed their
bodies together. The surf sprayed and ebbed, shifting
the sand and shells beneath them. They lay, half
covered with water, breathing hard.

"MacGregor?" he repeated suddenly, shaking his
head to clear it. Drops of water from his hair splattered
on her face. "Serena MacGregor?"

She pushed her own dripping hair out of her eyes and
tried to think. Her body was throbbing with the potent
combination of anger and desire. "Yes. And the moment I remember some of those wonderful Scottish
curses, I'm going to dump them all on you."

For the first time she saw pure surprise on his face. It
had the effect of draining her anger and replacing it
with bewilderment. Then his eyes narrowed on an
intense study of her features. Still panting, Serena
stared back, only to become more confused when the
smile spread slowly over his face. Dropping his forehead on hers, Justin chuckled, then roared with laughter.

The sound was appealing, but as she started to
respond to it, Serena concentrated on the uncomfortable lump of sand and shell digging into her back.
"What's so funny?" she demanded. "I'm soaking wet
and full of gritty sand. I've little doubt that my skin's
been slashed by shells and I never even finished my
lunch!"

Still laughing, he lifted his head, then gave her a
brotherly kiss on the nose. "Ask me again sometime.
Come on, let's rinse off and eat."

Chapter Three

Serena MacGregor. Justin shook his head as he reached into the narrow closet for a shirt. It was, he decided, the first time he'd been completely confounded in years. When a man made his living by his wits, he couldn't afford to be taken by surprise often.

Strange that he hadn't noticed the family resemblance, but then, she had little in common physically with her large, broad-featured, red-haired father. She was more a modern version of the little painted miniature Daniel kept in his library. How many times had he been to that fortress in Hyannis Port over the years? Justin wondered. Rena, as the family called her, had always been away at school. For some reason he had developed a picture of a scrawny, bespectacled scholar with Daniel's flaming hair and Anna's eccentric dignity. Yes, Serena MacGregor was quite a surprise.

Odd, he thought, that she would take a job that would do little more than pay her room and board when she was reputed to have an I.Q. that rivaled her father's weight and enough capital to buy an ocean liner for her personal pleasure yacht. Then again, the MacGregors were a strange, stubborn lot, prone to the unexpected.

For a moment Justin stood, naked from the waist, his shirt hanging forgotten from his fingertips. His torso was dark and lean, the skin stretched taut over his rib cage, where on the left it was marred by a six-inch scar. He was remembering.

The first time he had met Daniel MacGregor, Justin had been twenty-five. A run of luck had given him enough money to buy out his partner in their small hotel on the Strip in Las Vegas. Justin wanted to expand and remodel. For that he needed financing. Banks were usually dubious about lending large sums of money to men who made their living with a deck of cards. In any case, Justin didn't care for bankers, with their smooth hands and dry voices. And the Indian in him had little faith in a promise made on paper. Then he heard of Daniel MacGregor.

In his own fashion, Justin checked out the stock wizard and financier. He gained a picture of a tough, eccentric Scotsman who made his own rules, and won. Justin contacted him, diddled around by phone and letter for over a month, then made his first trip to the fortress in Hyannis Port.

Daniel worked out of his home. He didn't care for office buildings where one had to depend on elevators and secretaries. He'd purchased his plot of land near the sea with the wealth he had earned first with his back, and then with his mind. Daniel had realized early that he could earn more, very satisfactorily, with his mind. Then he had built his home and his empire—to his own liking.

It was a huge barn of a house, with massive corridors and enormous rooms. Daniel didn't like to be crowded. Justin's first impression of him as he was led into the tower room that served as his office was of bulk . . . and wit.

"So you're Blade." Daniel drummed his fingers on the surface of a desk that had been carved from a giant California redwood.

"Yes. And you're MacGregor."

A grin creased the broad face. "That I am. Sit down, boy." Daniel noticed no change of expression at his use of the term, and folded his hands over his chest as Justin sat. He liked the way Justin moved; he'd judged men on less. "So, you want a loan."

"I'm offering an investment, Mr. MacGregor," Justin corrected him coolly. The chair was designed to swallow a man. Justin sat in it with an ease that only accentuated the readiness to spring. "With my property as collateral, of course."

"Umm-hmm." Daniel steepled his hands as he continued to study the man across from him. Not a simple man, he concluded, observing the aristocratic features. Cool, controlled, and potentially violent. Comanche blood—warrior's blood—but not a brawler. Daniel came from good warrior stock himself. "Umm-hmm," he said again. "What are you worth, boy?"

An angry retort sprang to Justin's mind and was left

to smolder. Reaching down, he brought up a briefcase. "I have the financial papers, the appraisals, and so forth."

Daniel gave a gusty laugh and waved them away. "You think you'd have gotten this far if I didn't know all the figures you have in there? What about you?" he demanded. "Why should I lend my money to you?"

Justin set the briefcase back on the floor. "I pay my debts."

"Wouldn't last long in your business if you didn't."

"And I'll make you a great deal of money."

Daniel laughed again until his blue eyes watered. "I've got money, boy."

"Only a fool doesn't want more," Justin said quietly, and Daniel stopped laughing.

Leaning back in his chair, he nodded. "You're damn right." Then he grinned, slapping his wide palm on the desk. "You're damn right. How much to fix up that little hole in the wall of yours?"

"Three hundred and fifty thousand," Justin answered without blinking.

Daniel reached into his desk and drew out a bottle of Scotch and a deck of cards. "Stud poker."

They played for an hour, speaking only to bet. Justin heard the reverberating gong of a grandfather clock from somewhere deep in the house. Once someone knocked on the door. Daniel bellowed at them, and they weren't disturbed again. The scent of Justin's cigar mixed with the aroma of whiskey and the ripe fragrance of the overblown roses on the windowsill. After dropping fifteen hundred dollars, Daniel leaned back in his chair again.

"You'll need stockholders."

"I've just gotten rid of a partner." Justin crushed out the butt of his cigar. "I don't want another."

"Stockholders, boy." Daniel pushed the cards aside. "You want to make money, you've got to spread it around first. A man who plays like you do already knows that." With his pale blue eyes on Justin's, he considered a moment. "I'll lend you the money and buy in for ten percent. You're smart, you keep sixty and spread the rest around." After swirling the Scotch, he drained his glass and grinned. "You're going to be rich."

"I know."

Daniel's gusty laugh shook the windowpane. "Stay for dinner," he said, heaving himself out of his chair.

Justin stayed for dinner, and became rich. He renamed his hotel Comanche, then made it into one of the finest hotel-casinos in Vegas. He bought a dying property in Tahoe and repeated his success. Within a decade he had five thriving gambling hotels and interests in a variety of enterprises throughout the country and Europe. In the ten years since their meeting in the tower room, Justin had been to the MacGregor home dozens of times, entertained Daniel and Anna in his own hotels, and fished with their sons. But he'd never met the daughter.

"Bright girl," Daniel would say of her from time to time. "But won't settle down. Needs a good man—you should meet her."

And Justin had steered clear of the not so subtle matchmaking attempts. Or so he'd thought.

"The old devil," he murmured, shrugging into the shirt.

It had been Daniel who had pushed him into the cruise. Get away from the pressure, he'd insisted. Nothing like good sea air and half-naked women to relax a man. Because he'd been restless, Justin had considered it, then had been trapped when Daniel had mailed him the tickets with a request for a case of duty-free Scotch.

So the old pirate was still wheeling and dealing, Justin thought, amused. Daniel would have known that Justin would spend time in the casino on board, and had left the rest to chance. With a quick laugh Justin began doing up the buttons of his shirt. Chance, he reflected, with a stacked deck. What would the old man have to say if he knew his friend and business associate had been wrestling with his daughter that afternoon with the predominant notion of getting her into his bed? Exasperated, Justin ran a hand through his hair. Daniel MacGregor's daughter. Good God.

Justin grabbed a jacket from the closet, then closed it with a bang. It would serve the cagey devil right if he had seduced his daughter. It would serve him right if he avoided her for the rest of the trip and never uttered a word about meeting her in the first place. That would drive the Scotsman up the wall. Justin caught his own reflection in the mirror, a dark lean man in black and white.

"And if you think you can stay away from her, you're out of your mind," he muttered.

When he walked into the casino, Serena was standing near the small black and white monitor talking to the blond man Justin recognized as her supervisor. She laughed at something he said, then shook her head. Justin's eyes narrowed fractionally as Dale ran a finger down her cheek. He knew what it would feel like—soft and cool to the touch. Dale grinned, then straightened her bow tie as he spoke to her in undertones. Even recognizing the emotion as petty jealousy, Justin had trouble controlling it. In a matter of days Serena had made him feel desire, fury, and jealousy—emotions he normally kept in perfect balance. Cursing her father, he walked over to her.

"Serena." He caught the quick stiffening of her shoulders before she turned. "Not dealing tonight?"

"I've just come on from my break." She should have known the twenty-four-hour respite wouldn't last. "I didn't see you in here last night, I thought perhaps you'd fallen overboard." Hearing Dale's sharp indrawn breath, Serena turned back to him. "Dale, this is Justin Blade. When I didn't fall for his charm at the beach in Nassau, he tossed me into the water."

"I see." Dale extended his hand. "I've never tried that one. Did it work?"

"Shut up, Dale," Serena said sweetly.

"You'll have to excuse her," Dale told Justin. "Sea life makes some of us surly. Are you enjoying your trip, Mr. Blade?"

"Yes." Justin glanced at Serena. "It's been quite an experience so far."

"You will pardon me," she said with exaggerated politeness. "I have to relieve Tony." Turning, she stalked over to table five. Because gritting her teeth hurt her jaw, Serena forced the muscles to relax. She

gave the three players at the table a professional smile
which iced over as Justin took a vacant stool. "Good
evening. New deck." Breaking the seals, Serena shuf-
fled the cards together, doing her best to ignore Justin's
calm, steady stare. He stacked what she estimated to be
two hundred dollars worth of chips in the slot in front
of him, then lit a cigar. After giving the cards a final
snap, she determined to see if she could clean him
out.

"Cut?"

Justin took the thin sheet of plastic she offered. As
Serena slipped the cards into their clear holder, he
pushed a twenty-five-dollar marker forward. She
checked the table to see if all bets were placed, then
began.

At one point Serena had him down to three chips and
was feeling a grim satisfaction. Then she dealt him
double sevens, which he split, counting twenty on one
hand and twenty-one on the other. Steadily, he built
the five chips to ten. When it came time to rotate her
table, he infuriated her by moving with her. Serena
renewed her vow to clean him out.

For the next twenty minutes she hardly noticed the
other players. She could see only Justin's unfathomable
green eyes or his hand as he stood pat or took a hit.
Though she was determined to beat him, his chips
gradually multiplied.

"I got blackjack!" The shout from the college student at the end of the table broke her concentration.
Serena glanced over to see him grinning. "I won three
dollars!" he told the casino at large, holding up the
three light blue chips like a trophy. He was, Serena

concluded, pleasantly drunk. "Now . . ." He slapped the three chips back on the table, then rubbed his palms together. "I'm ready to gamble."

Laughing, she reached for the cards again, but her eyes met Justin's. She saw humor, the first expression she'd seen in them for hours, and warmed to it. For a moment she wanted to reach across the table and touch him, run her fingers through the thick soft hair that surrounded his lean face. How could the simple light of laughter in his eyes make him seem so important?

"Hey!" The college student lifted his beer in a toast. "I'm on a streak."

"Yeah, of one," his girlfriend said dryly.

The interruption cleared Serena's head. Lifting her chin, she reached for the cards. One smile wasn't going to make her forget she was here to beat him. "Possible blackjack," she said as she flipped over an ace for herself. "Insurance?" The college student's girlfriend plunked down a chip. Justin didn't move. Turning up the tip of her hole card, Serena was satisfied with a three. It would give her plenty of room. "No blackjack." She glanced at Justin's cards, pleased to have dealt him a poor count. "Sixteen. Hit or stand?" He merely motioned with his forefinger for a card. Serena had to bite back an oath as she turned over a four. "Twenty." He passed a hand over the cards to indicate he was satisfied.

And so you should be, she thought resentfully, turning up a jack to break the next player. Just freak luck, she told herself, bumping the college student up to eighteen. "Four or fourteen," she announced as she turned over her card. With her eyes on Justin's, she pulled another. "Six or sixteen," she said as if to him alone. She bit back another oath as she drew the three of clubs. "Dealer stands on nineteen," she stated, knowing Dale would throw her overboard if she took another hit. "Pays twenty."

Raking in all the chips but Justin's, she then slid another twenty-five-dollar marker over the baize. She thought she caught another glimpse of laughter in his eyes as he dropped it into his slot, but this time it didn't warm her.

Smoke hung in the air, too thick to be completely banished by the cooling system. Serena didn't need to glance at her watch to know she'd been standing on her feet for nearly ten consecutive hours. Gradually, the clatter from the slots began to lessen, the first indication that the late shift was almost over. The couple at the end of the table, looking heavy-eyed, began discussing the stopover in Puerto Rico the next day. Between them they cashed in five dollars worth of chips before they left.

A quick glance around showed Serena that all but three of the tables were empty. There were only two players left at hers, Justin and a woman she identified as the Mrs. Dewalter who had captured Jack's and Rob's attention. The redhead was paying a great deal more attention to Justin than to her cards. Feeling spiteful, Serena decided the diamond on her hand was vulgar, and nearly grinned when she broke her at twenty-three.

"I guess this isn't my game," the redhead said with a sulky pout. She shifted toward Justin so that her considerable cleavage was in full view. "You seem to be tremendously lucky. Do you have a system?" Running a finger down his sleeve, she smiled. Serena wondered how she would like her nose pressed into the green baize.

Amused at the obvious tactic, Justin allowed his eyes to roam up from the deep plunge of her bodice to her face. "No."

"You must have some secret," she murmured. "I'd love to hear it . . . over a drink?"

"I never drink when I play." He blew a stream of smoke past her shoulder. "One interferes with the other."

"Bets?" Serena said just a tad too sharply.

"I believe I've had enough cards this evening." Letting her thighs brush Justin's, she rose, then dropped a hundred dollars worth of chips into her purse. Serena had the small satisfaction of knowing she'd started with four. "I'll be in the lounge," she told Justin with a last lingering smile before she turned away.

"Better luck next time," Serena said before she could stop herself. She turned back to find Justin grinning at her.

"Cash me in?"

"Certainly." Then he'll go chasing after the redhead with the size 38C personality, she thought furiously. Quickly, she stacked and counted his chips. Seven hundred and fifty dollars, she calculated, and only became more angry. "Dale's busy, I'll take care of this myself."

Watching her stride away, Justin tried to remember her father. It wasn't easy.

Serena came back with a stack of crisp bills and a white slip attached to a clipboard. Swiftly, she counted the money out, then passed it across the table. "You had a profitable evening." After slipping the paper into the compartment under the table, she reached for the cards. Justin took her wrist.

"Another hand?" he asked, enjoying the quick jump of her pulse beneath his fingers.

"You've already cashed in," she pointed out, and tried to tug away. He tightened his grip.

"A different bet, between you and me."

"I'm sorry, it's against the rules to have side games with the passengers. Now, if you'll excuse me, I have to close up the table."

"No money." He watched her eyes narrow in fury and smiled. "A walk on the deck if I win," he said smoothly.

"Not interested."

"Not afraid to go one on one, are you, Serena?" The hand that attempted to remove his from her wrist paused. "You still have house advantage," he said quietly.

"If I win," she began, then carefully removed his hand, "you'll keep away from me for the rest of the cruise?"

He considered the question. It was, after all, a much wiser course than the one he was pursuing. Taking a last puff on his cigar, he crushed it out. It wouldn't be the first time he left his fate to the cards. "Deal."

He glanced at the two and five in front of him, then at the ten Serena had showing. Nodding for a hit, he drew a queen. His first thought was to stand, but another glance at Serena showed him she looked entirely too pleased with herself. He'd have bet every dollar in his pocket she had an eight or better in the hole. Keeping his eyes on hers, he gestured for another card.

"Damn!" She tossed down the four of diamonds and glared at him. "I swear, Justin, one day I'm going to beat you." Disgusted, she turned over the jack she had in the hole.

"No." He rose, slipping his hands into his pockets. "Because you're trying to beat me, not the cards. I'll wait for you outside."

Dale glanced over to see his best blackjack dealer sticking her tongue out at the back of a passenger.

Leaning back against the wall, Justin watched Serena through the glass doors of the casino. He thought he could almost see the combination of annoyance and frustration simmering around her. He felt much the same way himself. With a shrug he reminded himself that he had left it up to chance. The bet could have been as easily lost as won.

Idly, he fingered a twenty-five-dollar chip still in his pocket. Some might say he'd had an unusual run of luck. Then again, he mused, it might have been luckier to have lost that final bet. If he continued to see Serena, his life wasn't going to be uncomplicated.

He might have been able to ignore the feeling of having Daniel MacGregor looking over his shoulder if he could have convinced himself that taking her to bed would get her out of his system. But those were very long odds. She was the first woman Justin had ever known who had threatened to become a permanent part of his thoughts.

And what would she say, he wondered, if he told her her father had arranged the entire scenario from his fortress in Hyannis Port? A smile curved the corners of his mouth. She'd skin the old man and hang him up to dry, he concluded. Watching Serena walk toward the doors, Justin decided to save that little bombshell for another day.

"I suppose you have a right to smile," Serena said coolly as she let the door close behind her. "You're on quite a winning streak."

Justin took her hand, and in an unexpectedly courtly gesture kissed her fingers. "I intend for it to go on a lot longer before it's broken. You're really quite beautiful, Serena."

Disconcerted, she stared at him. "When I'm angry," she finished, struggling not to be charmed.

He turned her hand over and kissed her palm, watching her. "Really quite beautiful."

"Don't try to throw me off by being nice." Unconsciously, she laced her fingers with his. "There's nothing nice about you."

"No," he agreed. "Let's go out. I imagine you could use some fresh air."

"I agreed to take a walk." Together they began to climb the stairs. "That's all I agreed to."

"Umm-hmm. And the moon's nearly full. How'd you do tonight?"

"The casino?" When he opened the door the wind rushed in, delightfully warm and clean. "Better than usual. We've been operating at a loss since spring."

"Too many nickel slots—cuts your profit margin." He slipped an arm around her waist as Serena looked up at him. "You'd make more at the tables if some of your dealers were sharper."

"It's hard to stay sharp when you work up to sixty hours a week for peanuts," she said ruefully. "Anyway, the turnover's constant. Most of them have six weeks training tops, working up from cashier to croupier, and a large percentage of them don't stay more than a couple of runs because they find out it's not the floating vacation they thought it was." Without realizing it, she hooked her arm around his waist as he matched his stride to hers. "This is my favorite part."

"What?"

"Late at night when the ship's quiet. You can't hear anything but the sea. If I had a porthole in my cabin, I'd leave it open all night."

"No porthole?" His hand began to move rhythmically up and down her back.

"Only passengers and officers have outside cabins." She arched against his hand, sighing as it soothed her tired muscles. "Still, I wouldn't trade this past year for anything. It's been like finding a second family."

"Your family's important to you?" he asked, thinking of Daniel.

"Of course." Because she found it an odd question, Serena tilted her head back to look at him. As he angled his to meet her eyes, her lips nearly skimmed his jaw. "Don't do that," she murmured.

"What?" And the word, soft and quiet, whispered over her parted lips.

"You know very well what." Dropping her arm, she moved away from him toward the rail. "My family," she said more steadily as she turned, resting her arms across the wood, "has always been the most important part of my life. The loyalty is sometimes uncomfortably fierce, but necessary to all of us. What about you?"

She looked totally and unconsciously intriguing, her soft curves hidden, yet enhanced by the mannish tux, her once tidy hairstyle being whipped apart by the wind. Her face was tilted back so that a splash of moonlight marbleized her skin.

"My family . . ." Struggling to pick up the thread of the conversation, he moved to stand in front of her. "I have a sister, Diana. She's ten years younger; we've never been close."

"Your parents?"

"They died when I was sixteen. Diana went to live with an aunt. I don't think I've seen her in practically twenty years."

Serena's automatic wave of sympathy was immediately quelled. "That's disgraceful!"

"My aunt's never approved of my profession," he said dryly. Though she never questions the money for Diana's support, he mused, moving his hands to the buttons of Serena's jacket. "It was easier for Diana if I didn't interfere."

"What right does your aunt have to approve or disapprove?" Serena demanded, too inflamed to notice how deftly he was unbuttoning her jacket. "She's your sister.'

"My aunt's a firm believer that gambling is the devil's work. She's a Grandeau, from the French part of the family."

Serena shook her head at his logic. "So what are you?"

"Blade." His eyes locked on hers. "Comanche."

His face was very close, closer than she had realized. Though she felt the wind flutter through the thin fabric of her shirt, she didn't yet understand what he had done. Serena found herself swallowing as his eyes held hers. Had there been a threat in those two words, or had it been her imagination?

"I should have known," she managed. "I suppose I let your eyes throw me off."

"From the drops of French and Welsh blood that slipped through. My father was almost pure, and my mother descended from the line of a Comanche brave and a French settler." Slowly, his eyes never leaving hers, he pulled loose the tie at her throat. Serena swallowed again, but didn't move. "The story goes that one of my ancestors saw a woman with golden hair alone near a creek bed. She had a basket of laundry and was singing as she washed. He was a fierce warrior who had killed many of her people to protect his land. When he saw her, he wanted her." Justin released the buttons of her blouse, one by one. "So he took her."

"That's barbaric," she managed over a suddenly dry throat. "He kidnapped her, stole her away from her family—"

"A few days later she sunk a knife into his shoulder, trying to escape," Justin continued quietly. "But when she saw his blood on her hands, she didn't run. She stayed and nursed him and gave him green-eyed sons and daughters."

"Perhaps it took more courage to stay than to use the knife."

Justin smiled, noting the tremor in her voice and the

steadiness of her eyes. "He gave her a name that translates to Prize of Gold and never took another woman. So it's a tradition, when one of my people sees a woman with golden hair who he wants—he takes."

His mouth crushed down on hers, whirling her quickly into passion. With his hands he dove into her hair, dislodging pins that danced in the wind before they fell into the waves below. Serena grabbed his shoulders, almost afraid she would follow them, plunging down into the dark, fast water. For surely this was how it felt to spiral down, helpless, from a high point toward the unknown. Her heart was racing even before his palm covered it, a contact of hard flesh against soft—man against woman.

On a moan she tightened her grip, as if he were a life line in a sea that had gone suddenly from calm to tumultuous. Forgetting her smallness, he took her into his hand, abandoning both gentleness and reason. No man had ever dared touch her that way; perhaps that was why she allowed it. He dared, without request, without practiced words of seduction. It was a force, consuming them both—an impulse too old and too basic to be denied.

Her body throbbed to be touched. While her thoughts tangled, it took over, showing them both what she needed. The wild, ruthless kisses that raced down her throat only made her crave more. The warm, soothing breeze from the sea became like small flames to heighten her fever. She drew the moist air into her lungs and felt it turn to fire.

The hand at her breast kneaded, tormented, while the other slipped up her naked back to find some tiny point near her spine. A press of his finger turned her legs to jelly. She gasped as she arched against him while waves of unbelievable pleasure ran through her.

"No." Serena's voice sounded thin and far off. "No, don't."

But he pressed his lips to hers to devour her trembling protest. Her mouth was too hungry to heed the warning that had sounded in her brain. It clung to his, relishing the light flavor of salt spray. Whatever magic his fingers held, it dominated her now. She would give anything he asked, so long as he never stopped touching her. Digging her hands into his hair, she dragged him closer without noticing the fine mist of dampness that lay on it.

When her lips were free, with his buried at her throat, she could do no more than breathe his name. The moistness on her face went unfelt; all her senses were bound up in what his hands and lips could bring her. Then he was moving, and she swayed as he took her away from the rail. Weak with desire, Serena leaned against him while he stroked her hair.

"You're getting drenched," Justin murmured, but couldn't prevent his lips from brushing over the damp crown of her head, couldn't prevent himself from breathing in its fragrance. "Let's go in."

"What?" Dazed, Serena opened her eyes and saw the fine curtain of rain. "It's raining?" As the cool water revived her she shook her head. She felt she had been in a dream, to be wakened by a brisk slap in the face. "I—" Pushing away from him, she ran a hand through her hair. "I . . ."

"Have to get some sleep," he finished. He had come

too close, Justin discovered, to taking her, like a maniac, where they had stood.

"Yes." Feeling raindrops on her bare flesh, Serena clutched her jacket together. "Yes, it's late." Her eyes were still clouded and confused as she glanced around the deck. "It's raining," she repeated.

There was something about her abrupt vulnerability that made Justin want her more than he had moments before, and made it impossible to take her. Sticking his hands into his pockets, he balled them briefly into fists. Damn Daniel MacGregor, he thought fiercely. The Scotsman set a fine trap with prime bait. If he took her now, it would almost certainly destroy his relationship with a man he'd come close to loving. If he didn't, he would only go on wanting her. If he waited . . . well, that was the gamble.

"Good night, Serena."

She stood irresolute a moment, wanting to race inside to sanity, wanting to fall into his arms and madness. Taking a deep breath, she clutched her jacket tighter. "Good night."

Serena went quickly, knowing it took only a moment to change a mind.

Chapter Four

Because she thought it would be deserted, Serena chose the Veranda deck aft. Anyone still on board would more likely opt for the larger pool area, with its proximity to the Lido Bar and Grill, for sunning. Most of the passengers would be seeing the sights in San Juan, walking the bricked streets in the historical section, exploring forts, snapping pictures of the surrounding mountains. Anyone who dribbled back during the day wasn't likely to disturb her on the quiet rear deck.

She'd nearly overslept, forgetting she was slated to help Dale figure last night's take. Because it had been dawn before Serena had finally drifted off, she'd managed only four hours sleep before the alarm had shocked her awake. With her work finished for the morning, she'd come to lie in the midday sun and bake the tiredness from her body.

Serena didn't want to think, as she had during those long quiet hours between three A.M. and dawn. She knew she was too weary to dwell on what had happened the previous evening, but even as she stretched out on a deck chair, everything came back to play in her head. What was it that happened to her every time Justin's lips touched hers? Whatever it was, Serena had sworn she wouldn't let it happen again, then had been helpless to prevent it. What was it about him that kept pulling her along, dragging her closer to the edge of something fatal? Each time it became more difficult to remember to back away.

Serena released the halter strings to the top of her bikini and settled back. It might be smarter all in all, she decided, to give the whole business some serious thought rather than to dance around it. If there was one common thread running through the MacGregor clan, it was that they were realists. Face a problem head-on and mow it down. That, Serena thought with a quick grin, should have been their clan motto. So, for the problem of Justin Blade.

He was dangerously attractive. Dangerous, Serena concluded, because the attraction had hit her in the first instant and hadn't abated in the least. And it wasn't merely his looks, she mused, adjusting her sunglasses. Looks could easily be discounted. It was that strength and the sex, and the quietly domineering style. All three challenged her to match him, point for point. It was, very simply, an irresistible combination to a woman who rarely chose the easy path.

Did she like him? Serena gave an automatic snort, then became thoughtful. Well, she asked herself again, *did* she? The answer came with the memories of an easy afternoon in Nassau, that quick, shared joke in the casino, the natural way her hand fit with his. Perhaps she did like him, Serena admitted uncomfortably. A little. But, she pushed her sunglasses more firmly on her nose and shut her eyes, that wasn't the point. The point was, what was she going to do about him for the next five days?

She couldn't hide. Even if it had been physically possible while they were both on the same ship, Serena's pride would never have allowed it. No, she would have to deal with him . . . and with herself. The idea that she could spend some time with him, learn to know him a bit better, could no longer be classified as harmless. If she were honest, Serena would have to admit that she had known from the outset that there was nothing harmless about Justin Blade. That took her full circle, back to the basic attraction. And this, she decided as she rolled over onto her stomach, wasn't solving anything.

She had only a few more days aboard the *Celebration* before she headed home for an extended visit. Unemployed. Wrinkling her nose, she shifted until she was comfortable on the thick plastic strips of the lounge. With the rest of her life to decide upon, what to do about an encounter with an itinerant gambler should hardly take precedence in her thoughts. It was only, Serena concluded, because she was allowing it to. Now that she had admitted that she found Justin both attractive and interesting, that should be the end of it.

Her course was really quite simple—treat him as she would treat any other passenger. Polite and friendly. Well, she amended, dropping her sunglasses on the deck, not too friendly. And no more side bets, Serena added firmly before she shut her eyes. The man's luck was phenomenal.

And the sun was much too warm, the deck much too quiet to think about complications. Sighing, she pillowed her head on her hands and slept.

Warm and soothing . . . These sensations drifted through her, causing Serena to sigh again. Hazy thoughts of floating naked on a raft while the sun stroked her skin brought a small sound of pleasure to her lips. She could have floated endlessly, without destination. She felt a freedom—no, an abandonment. She was alone in a blue sea, or perhaps in a dense green jungle. A secret, solitary place where there were no restrictions. There the sun caressed her body like lover's hands.

She could feel its stroking, bringing hot, sleepy pleasure . . . languid fingers of sunlight . . . lazily arousing . . . delicately seducing. . . .

The brush of a butterfly against her ear made her smile. Serena lay still, not wanting to disturb it. Soft as dew, it fluttered to her cheek, resting a moment, as though it had found a pungent blossom. With a final sweep of wings it whispered her name at the corner of her mouth.

How strange, she thought with a tiny moan of pleasure, for a butterfly to know her name. Shifting her shoulders toward the gentle caress on her back, Serena commanded her eyes to open, wanting to see the colors of those soft wings. She saw only the cool depthless green of Justin's eyes.

For a moment Serena stared into them, too content to be confused. "I thought you were a butterfly," she murmured as she closed her eyes again.

"Did you?" Smiling, Justin touched his lips to the corner of hers a second time.

"Mmm-hmm." It came out as a long, lazy sigh. "How did you get here?"

"Where?" Enjoying her gentle stretching beneath his palm, he continued to stroke her back.

"Wherever we are," Serena murmured. "Did you float on a raft?"

"No." He knew from the rhythm of her breathing, by that brief look into her dark, misty eyes, that she was already aroused, disoriented enough to be completely pliant. Her absolute vulnerability touched off twin urges to take and to protect. As each one fought for supremacy, Justin brushed a kiss over her bare shoulder. "You've been dreaming."

"Oh." Serena didn't see why it mattered as long as those wonderful, warm caresses continued. "It feels good."

"Yes." Justin traced a fingertip down her spine. "It does."

The touch brought a quick shudder, a more concentrated arousal. Serena's eyes flew open. "Justin?"

"Yes?"

Abruptly awake and throbbing, Serena lifted herself up on her elbows. "What are you doing here?"

Briefly, his eyes passed over the small swatch of material that tenuously clung to her breasts. "You already asked me that. With your skin you shouldn't lie in the sun unprotected." He slid his hand down her back, spreading the cream he'd applied. When his fingers pressed near the base of her spine, she caught her breath.

"Stop it!" she demanded, furious that her voice was shaky.

"You're very sensitive," he murmured. The desire in her eyes had flared quickly, darkening and widening even as she struggled against it. "It seems a pity we're never at the appropriate spot at the appropriate time."

"Justin." Serena shifted away from his hand, barely remembering to hold the top of her bikini in place. "I really wish you'd let me get some rest." As she sat up, she meticulously tied her halter strings behind her neck. "I had to get up early this morning, and the casino opens as soon as we leave port tonight." Stretching out again, she dismissed him. "I want a nap."

"I want to talk to you." He shifted lightly on the balls of his feet where he had crouched beside her, then rose.

"Well, I don't—" She broke off as her gaze traveled up long muscular legs to narrow hips encased in brief black trunks, to a hard, lean torso. It was a body that hinted at strength and sinew and speed. Quickly, Serena averted her gaze, reaching behind her to adjust the back of the deck chair. "I don't want to talk to you," she finished, popping her sunglasses back on her nose. "Why don't you go visit San Juan like everyone else?"

"I have a proposition."

"I bet you do."

Without waiting for an invitation, Justin nudged her legs over and sat on the end of the chair. "Business."

Serena slid her legs farther away so that her skin wouldn't rub against his and distract her. "I'm not interested in your business. Go get your own chair."

"Isn't there a rule about crew being rude to passengers?"

"Report me," she invited him. "It's my last week on the job."

"That's what I want to talk to you about." Justin ran a lotion-slick palm along her thigh.

"Justin—"

"Good." He smiled at her furious face. "I have your attention."

"You're going to have a fractured nose if you don't leave me alone," she told him, exasperated.

"Do you always have such a difficult time concentrating on a business discussion?" Justin asked mildly.

"Not a legitimate one."

"Then we shouldn't have any problem."

Flopping back on the chair, Serena eyed him from behind the tinted glasses. She spotted the jagged white scar along his ribs. "That looks as if it was nasty," she said with a cool smile. "A present from a jealous husband?"

"A bigot with a knife." His answer was as cool as her question, and devoid of emotion.

A pain shot into her, sharp and unexpected. It caught with a gasp in her throat as she could almost see the blade slicing into flesh. "That was a stupid thing to say. I'm sorry." She glanced at the scar again, nearly sick from her own careless words. "It must've been serious."

Justin thought of the drugged two weeks in the hospital ward, then shrugged. "It was a long time ago."

"What happened?" She couldn't prevent herself from asking, perhaps because some intimate part of her shared the pain without knowing the cause.

Justin studied her for a moment. He didn't think about the incident anymore. Perhaps he hadn't given it more than a cursory thought in fifteen years. Still it was, like the scar, a part of him. It might be better if she knew. Taking a towel from the deck, he wiped his hands.

"I was in a bar in eastern Nevada. One of the regulars didn't care to breathe the same air as an Indian. I had a beer to finish, so I suggested he breathe somewhere else." A very cold, mirthless smile touched his mouth. "I was young enough to find some enjoyment in the prospect of a brawl. At eighteen a fistfight relieves a lot of frustrations."

"But you didn't get that scar from a fistfight," she murmured.

Justin lifted a brow in acknowledgment. "Most things tend to get out of hand when liquor's involved. He was drunk and feeling mean." Almost absently, he ran a finger down the line of the scar in a habitual gesture he thought he'd conquered years before. "It started predictably enough—words, shoves, fists—then he had a knife. He was probably too drunk to realize what he was doing, but he had it into me."

"Oh, God." Automatically, Serena reached out to

take his hand. "That's horrible. Why didn't someone call the police?"

It flashed through his mind that despite the wealth, the extensive education, and traveling, she'd lived a sheltered life—perhaps because of it. "Things aren't always done that way," he said simply.

"But he *stabbed* you," she said with a mixture of logic and revulsion. "He must have been arrested."

"No." Justin's gaze remained as calm and steady as his voice. "I killed him."

At the flat statement, Serena's hand went limp in his. Justin could see her eyes grow wide and shocked behind the tinted glasses. He felt her instant, automatic withdrawal. Then just as quickly, her fingers tightened on his again. "In self-defense," she said with only a trace of a tremor in her voice.

He said nothing. All those years ago he had needed that kind of simple, unquestioning faith—during the pain of his hospital days, the cold, solitary fear in his cell awaiting trial. There'd been no one then to believe in him. No one to give him back any portion of the hope and trust he had lost during those endless, empty days. As she cupped his hand between both of hers, something moved inside him and crept out of a long-closed lock.

"I grabbed for the knife," Justin said at length. "We fell. The next thing I knew I was waking up in the hospital, charged with second-degree murder."

"But it was his knife." There was quick outrage in her voice and no question. "He attacked you."

"It took a while for that to come out." Justin could

remember every hour, every minute of the waiting—
the smell of the cell, the faces in the courtroom. The
fear and fury. "When it did, I was acquitted."

With how many other scars? Serena wondered. "No
one wanted to testify for you," she said instinctively.
"The others in the bar that night."

"I wasn't one of them," he said flatly. "But they
stuck to the truth when they were under oath."

"It must have been a frightening experience for a boy
to go through." When Justin only lifted a brow, Serena
tried to find a smile. "My father would say that a man's
not a man until he's thirty, or maybe it's forty. He isn't
always consistent."

How well he knew, Justin thought. He was tempted
to tell her then and there about his relationship with
Daniel, but made himself stick with his original plan.
Justin Blade was consistent. "I told you about this
because if you accept my offer, you'd probably hear
snatches of it anyway. And I'd rather you had it from
me all at once." He saw that he had her curiosity now,
which was better than her attention.

"What kind of offer?" she asked warily.

"A job."

"A job?" Serena repeated, then laughed. "What do
you want to do, set up a floating blackjack game with
me as dealer?"

"I had something a bit more stationary in mind,"
Justin murmured as his eyes drifted down. "Just how
secure are those skinny little strings?"

"Secure enough." She barely resisted the urge to tug
at them. "Why don't you tell me exactly what you have
in mind, Justin. . . . Straight."

"All right." Abruptly, the humor left his eyes. They were cool again and level on hers. "I've watched you work. You're very good. Not just with the cards, but with people. You're a quick judge of the players, and your table is nearly always full, while some of the others thin out regularly. In addition to that, you know how to handle a player when he's annoyed with the cards or had a bit too much to drink. All in all," he added in the same impersonal tone, "you've got a lot of style."

Not certain what he was leading up to, and not wanting to be too pleased by his words, Serena moved her shoulders carelessly. "So?"

"So. I've a use for someone with your talents." His expression didn't change when her eyes narrowed. Justin merely folded his legs under him and watched her, looking, Serena thought, a bit too much like his infamous kidnapping ancestor must have looked.

Pushing her glasses on top of her head, Serena stared straight back at him. "What sort of use?" she asked coolly.

"Managing my casino in Atlantic City." He had the satisfaction of seeing incredulity cover her face.

"You own a casino in Atlantic City?"

Without seeming to move at all, Justin rested his hands lightly on his knees. "Yes."

Serena frowned at him through narrowed eyes. He thought, amused, that her trust didn't come as easily this time, then slowly she let out a breath. "Comanche," Serena murmured. "There's one in Vegas, too, and in Tahoe, I think." Leaning back, she closed her eyes. So the itinerant gambler turned out to be a very wealthy, very successful businessman. "I should have known."

Even more amused by her reaction, Justin relaxed. He'd first thought of offering her a job during their morning in Nassau. Then it had been part whim, part business. Studying her strong, elegant face, he knew it was already more than that, more than it should be. That was something he would deal with—after he'd arranged things.

"I fired my manager just before I left," Justin went on, not waiting for Serena to open her eyes again. "A bit of trouble with the take."

She opened them now, her brows arching. "He cheated you?"

"Tried," Justin corrected her mildly. "No one cheats me."

"No," Serena agreed. "I'm sure they don't." She drew her knees up so that they would no longer be touching, then wrapped her arms around them. "Why do you want me to work for you?"

Justin had the uncomfortable feeling she knew it was more than he'd said, even though he himself wasn't certain of all the reasons. He was only sure that he wanted her in his world where he could see . . . and touch her. "I've told you," he said simply, too cautious to stroke her skin again.

"If you have three successful hotels—"

"Five," he corrected her.

"Five." She gave him a slight nod. "Then I can't imagine you as a man who runs his business on impulse." Or anything else on impulse, she added silently. "You must know that managing a casino like yours is a long way from dealing cards on a cruise liner. You probably have twice the tables we do, and a take that would make our little profit look like bubble-gum money."

Justin allowed himself a smile. It was true enough. "Of course, if you don't think you can handle it—"

"I didn't say I couldn't handle it," she retorted, then scowled at him. "You're very clever, aren't you?"

"Think about it," he suggested, hooking his finger around one of hers. "You said yourself you have no definite plans after this cruise."

No definite plans, she mused. Just a vague notion about opening her own place. She still wanted her own place, but wouldn't it be logical to manage someone else's until she learned a bit more? "I'll think about it," Serena said slowly, hardly noticing that Justin's thumb was moving lightly up and down the length of her finger.

"Good." With his free hand he reached up, idly plucking a pin from her hair. "We can have dinner in San Juan and discuss the practicalities." Letting the first pin drop, Justin drew out another.

"Will you stop that." Annoyed, Serena grabbed his wrist. "Every time I see you, you're tossing my pins away. I won't have one left by the end of the cruise."

"I like it down." He ran his fingers through the loosely secured bun and scattered the rest of the pins. "I like to see it fall down."

Shoving his hand away, Serena scrambled up. When he used that tone, a smart woman kept her distance. "I'm not having dinner with you in San Juan or anywhere else." She snatched up the dashiki she'd worn over her suit. "And I believe I've thought long enough about your proposition."

`"Afraid?" Unfolding his legs, Justin rose in a smooth, catlike movement.

"No." She met his eyes calmly, so that he would understand she spoke the truth.

"Good." Pleased with the strong, stubborn look, he cupped his hand around the base of her neck. Fear was too ordinary and too easily defeated. "But take a few days to think this over. The business offer is exactly that. It has nothing to do with you and me being lovers."

The firm kneading of his fingers at the back of her neck had nearly seduced her into relaxing. His words had her eyes flashing. "We're not lovers."

"We will be," he said, holding her still with one hand as he stepped closer. "Soon. We're both people who take what we want, Serena. We want each other."

"Why don't you put your ego down for a while, Justin. It must be getting heavy." When his hand went to her lotioned back to press her closer, she remained stiff, unwilling to struggle, unwilling to lose.

"Gamblers believe in fate." Though her back was straight and unyielding, he felt the soft give of her breasts against his chest. Only a narrow band of material separated flesh from flesh. "You're as much a gambler as I am, Serena MacGregor." Lowering his head, he nibbled along her jawline. "We've both got to play with the hand we were dealt."

How long could she resist that honeyed tone and clever mouth? Already Serena could feel the hammer of her heart against her ribs and the heavy fluid weakness in her limbs. If she resisted, she would lose. Perhaps . . . Her brain began to cloud, and frantically she forced the silken mists away. Perhaps this time she would play the game his way and earn a draw. Fighting her own need to surrender, she took a dangerous gamble.

Slowly, softly, she ran her hands up his naked back, letting her fingernails lightly rake his skin. When his mouth pressed against her throat, her knees nearly buckled, but she bit down hard on the inside of her lip. Pain would help her keep control. She rubbed against him sinuously, while her fingers crept up to trace patterns on the base of his neck. His heartbeat began to thud, racing with hers.

His mouth grew hungry, but she turned so that his lips fell anywhere but on hers. If he kissed her, locked her in one of those deep, mindless feasts of mouth on mouth, she'd be lost. His breath raged unsteadily over her ear, wrenching a moan from her. Serena squeezed her eyes tightly, struggling not to feel all the things he could so effortlessly make her feel. She pressed her lips to his throat, telling herself it wasn't for the taste of him but only the next step in the game. She wouldn't be weakened by the dark male flavor, by the feel of muscle taut and strong under her hands. This time—this time, she promised herself, she'd bring him to his knees.

She heard him groan, felt the light quiver run through him as he crushed her against him. Too astonished by the newly discovered power to be pleased with it, Serena merely clung. He whispered something low, in a primitive tongue she didn't understand, before he buried his face in her hair.

Her heart urged her to stay as she was, warmed flesh to warmed flesh. Could it feel so right if she didn't belong there? If her body had not been fashioned for his, could they fit together so unerringly? If her mouth had not been made for his, would it heat at even the thought of a kiss?

No. Serena caught herself before the weakness could spread too far. She wouldn't let herself be ruled by a need . . . or by a man.

She pushed firmly away, knowing she was free only because she'd caught him off guard. Slowly, praying her legs would hold her, she bent down to retrieve the dashiki which had fallen to the deck. Without a word Serena slipped it over her head. It gave her a moment, just a moment, to brace herself before she looked at him.

She saw desire—a reckless desire that had her heart thudding painfully—in his eyes. And she saw the wariness. It strengthened her to know he'd been no more prepared for the attack on the senses than she had been. Because of it, she had the edge.

"If and when I decide I want to make love with you, you'll know." She said it calmly, then turned and walked away without a backward glance. Her knees were shaking.

Justin watched her. Oh, he could drag her back, he thought as his hand curled into a fist. He could drag her to his cabin and have her within a matter of moments. He could say the hell with the game plan and assuage this gnawing hunger that seemed to be eating him from the inside out. If once, just once, he was truly alone with her . . . With care Justin unclenched his hand. It never paid to let emotions rule your moves. That was something he'd learned too many years ago to forget now.

Bending, he picked up the bottle of lotion Serena had left beside her chair. She'd been intrigued with his offer, he mused, absently tightening the cap. And while she might try to shrug it off, the idea had been planted. After a year of following orders, the notion of giving them would appeal to her. Having come fresh from a victory, she would consider herself well able to handle him on the personal front. He counted on there being enough MacGregor in her to make a challenge irresistible.

A slow, cool smile touched his mouth. Justin was just as susceptible to a challenge as Serena. He'd made his bid, he decided. For the moment, he'd let it stand.

Serena's room was completely dark when the phone beside her bunk shrilled. Blindly, she groped about, fumbling for the button of the alarm. When this did nothing to stop the ringing, she pushed at it in annoyance, then knocked the receiver from the phone. It conked her smartly against the temple.

"Ouch, damn it!"

"Good morning, little girl."

Hazy with sleep and rubbing her head, she cradled the receiver against her ear. "Dad?"

"How's life on the high seas?" he asked in a booming, cheerful voice that made her wince.

"I—um . . ." Running her tongue over her teeth, Serena struggled to wake up.

"Come on, girl, speak up."

"Dad, it's . . ." She pushed at her alarm again until she could read the luminous dial. "It's barely six A.M."

"A good sailor's up with the dawn," he told her.

"Uh-huh. Good night, Dad."

"Your mother wants to know when you'll be home."

Even half asleep, Serena grinned. Anna MacGregor had never been a mother hen, but Daniel . . . "We'll be in Miami Saturday afternoon. I should be home by Sunday. Are you going to have a brass band?"

"Hah!"

"One Highland chief with a bagpipe?"

"You were always the sassy one, Rena." He tried to sound stern, and ended up sounding proud. "Your mother wants to know if they're feeding you proper."

She swallowed a giggle. "We get a whole loaf of barley bread a week and salt pork on Sundays. How is Mom?"

"Fine. She's already gone to the hospital to cut somebody open."

"Alan and Caine?"

Daniel gave a snort. "Who sees them?" he demanded. "It breaks your mother's heart that her children've forgotten their parents. Not one grandchild to bounce on her knee."

"Inconsiderate of us," Serena agreed dryly.

"Now, if Alan had married that pretty Judson girl . . ."

"She walked like a duck," Serena reminded him bluntly. "Alan'll pick his own wife when he's ready."

"Hah!" Daniel said again. "Got his nose buried down in D.C., Caine's still sowing oats he should've been done with, and you float around on some boat."

"Ship."

"Your poor mother will never live to hold her first grandchild." With a heavy sigh he lit one of the fat cigars Anna hadn't managed to confiscate.

"Did you wake me up at six A.M. to lecture me about the procreation of the MacGregor line?"

"That's nothing to curl your lip at, little girl. The clan—"

"I'm not curling my lip," she assured him, wanting to avoid a long, passionate diatribe. "And I plan to stay home awhile, so you can start bullying me after Sunday."

"Now, is that any way to talk?" he demanded, offended. "Why, I've never so much as raised my hand to you."

"You're the best father I've ever had," she said soothingly. "I'll buy you a case of Scotch in St. Thomas."

"Well, now." Pleased with the idea, he softened, then remembered another promised case of Scotch and his main purpose for the predawn call. "Met any interesting people on the cruise, Rena?"

"Mmm, I could write a book. I'm really going to miss the rest of the crew."

"What about passengers?" he persisted. Daniel puffed on his cigar and tried his hand at smoke rings. "Get any real gamblers?"

"Now and again." Her thoughts drifted to Justin, just as Daniel's did.

"I suppose you've had your hands full with the men." She gave a noncommittal grunt and shifted to her back. One man anyway, she mused. "'Course there's nothing wrong with a bit of romance now and then," he added in a jovial voice. "Providing the man's got good blood and some starch. A true gambler has to have a sharp brain."

"Would you feel better if I told you I was planning to run off with one?"

"Which one?" he demanded, narrowing his eyes.

"No one," Serena returned firmly. "Now, I'm going back to sleep. Be sure to get rid of all that cigar ash before Mom gets home." Daniel scowled at the phone, then at the butt in his hands. "I'll see you and Mom Sunday. And by the way, I love you, you old pirate."

"Eat a decent breakfast," he ordered before he hung up.

Thoughtfully, Daniel leaned back in his massive chair. Rena had always been a tough egg to crack, he mused. As for Justin, well, if Justin Blade hadn't made it his business to spend a tropical evening or two in her company, then he wasn't the man Daniel thought he was. He tapped out his cigar, reminding himself to dispose of the evidence before Anna came home.

Damned if he was wrong about Justin Blade! Daniel MacGregor knew the make of a man. He gave himself a moment's pleasure speculating about a black-haired, violet-eyed grandchild. A boy first, he decided. Though he wouldn't carry the MacGregor name—and that was a pity—he'd carry MacGregor blood. They'd name him after his grandfather.

In a fine mood, Daniel picked up the phone, thinking he might as well badger his other children while he was at it.

Chapter Five

As much as she told herself it wasn't any of her business, Serena couldn't help wondering what Justin was up to. For two days she hadn't had a glimpse of him. During that time he hadn't set foot inside the casino. Nor had he been on the port side of the Promenade deck indulging in one of the private games, at least not when she just happened to stroll out there during her break.

What, Serena demanded of herself as she prepared for her last free day of the cruise, was he doing? A gambler was supposed to gamble, wasn't he? He wasn't the kind to settle for a bingo game in the lounge.

He's doing it on purpose, she decided as she buttoned up her scarlet romper. He's trying to get to me. She wouldn't have been the least surprised if while she had been working and wondering, he had spent his time lazing in the sun somewhere, knowing it. Infuriating. He'd probably had that cozy little drink with Mrs. Dewalter, too, she concluded, and grabbed her brush. Taking it through her hair in hard, quick strokes, Serena scowled at herself in the small mirror.

"So what?" she said aloud. "If he's nipping around her ankles, he's not nipping around mine." The last thing she'd wanted on her final days on the ship was a constant battle, verbal or otherwise. So it was just as well that he'd found something else to keep him occupied; that saved her the trouble of ignoring him.

He stirred her up when he was around. He stirred her up when he wasn't around, too, she thought, and tossed the brush back on the dresser. Where was the justice? I won't think about it, Serena decided, flopping down on the floor to slip on her sandals. I'm going to do some snorkeling, buy some trinkets—a case of Scotch—and, she added grimly, I'm going to enjoy myself. I won't give him another thought.

It's deliberate, she thought, slapping a sandal against her palm. He dangled that business about managing his casino in front of my nose, then disappeared. He knew it would drive me crazy, she decided with fresh frustration. Well, two can play, Serena reminded herself as she wiggled her foot into the sandal. I'll stay out of his way for the next couple of days if I have to claim seasickness and lock myself in my cabin. And that, she determined, would be a lesson to him.

Serena continued to frown when the knock sounded on her door. "It's open," she called shortly.

The last person she'd expected to see in her doorway

was Justin. The last thing she'd expected to feel was pleasure. Oh, my God, she realized, I've missed him.

He saw the quick smile light in her eyes before she successfully turned it into a glare. "'Morning."

"Passengers aren't permitted on this deck," she told him in a tone that was both cool and prim.

"Oh." He stepped inside, shutting the door behind him. Ignoring her hiss of annoyance, Justin glanced around the tiny cabin.

It should have been drab and colorless, with its plain bunk and white walls, but she'd given it an odd sort of style with only a few touches. A flashy painting of sailboats, a bottle-green free-form bowl filled with crushed shells, a boldly striped needlepoint pillow that reminded him of Anna. The pantry in Hyannis Port, he mused, was larger.

"No wasted space," he ventured, letting his eyes roam back to her.

"It's *my* space," Serena reminded him. "And it's strictly against the rules for you to be in here. Would you go away before you get me fired?"

"You've already quit." Easing between her and the bunk, Justin took a closer look at the painting. "This is very good—the harbor here in St. Thomas?"

"Yes." Serena stayed seated deliberately, knowing it was next to impossible for two people to stand in the cabin without touching. "I'm sorry I can't entertain you, Justin, but I'm just on my way out."

With an absent sound of agreement, he sat on the bunk. "Sturdy," he commented, nudging a reluctant smile from her. It was hard as a rock.

"It's great for the back." They sat eyeing each other for a moment as she fought off the simple pleasure of having him with her. "I thought I was rid of you."

"Did you?" Lifting the flimsy teddy she'd slept in, Justin ran the lace through his fingers. Without any effort he could picture her in it, picture the thin, creamy material sliding over her skin as he slipped it off of her.

"Put that down." She leaned over to snatch it out of his hands, going across his body to do so.

"So you have a taste for silk and lace," he stated, letting the lingerie slip back to the bed before Serena could grab it. "I've always admired women who wear things like this, then sleep alone." Justin looked down at her as Serena knelt on the floor, frustrated. "It shows a certain independence of spirit."

Her brow furrowed. "Is that a compliment?"

"I thought so." With a smile he leaned forward to wrap the ends of her hair around his fingers. "Why did you think you were rid of me?"

"I wish you wouldn't be nice, Justin; it throws me off." Sitting back on her haunches, Serena sighed. "You haven't been in the casino."

"There are other entertainments on board."

"I'm sure." Her voice chilled. "Like explaining your system to Mrs. Dewalter."

"Mrs. who?"

Her feathers ruffled, Serena got up and began to search for her tote bag. "The divorced redhead with the hen's egg."

"Oh." Amused and baffled, Justin watched her rummage under the bunk. "Looking for something?"

"Yes."

As he watched, Serena squirmed under the bunk on her stomach. "Would you like some help?"

"No. Damn it!" She swore as she rapped the back of her head on the bottom of the bunk. When she wiggled back out, Justin was sitting on the floor beside her. Without speaking, he smiled and brushed her mussed hair away from her face. "Justin . . ." Serena turned away and dumped the contents of the bag on the bunk. "I really hate to say this."

Accustomed to her sharp tongue, he shrugged. "Go ahead, say it anyway."

"I missed you."

Looking back, Serena saw surprise on his face for the second time. "I told you I hated to say it." When she started to rise, he took her arm and held her still.

Three words. Three words that brought on a torrent of conflicting emotions that he'd never experienced. He'd been prepared for her annoyance, her coolness, her fury. But not for those three simple words. "Serena." He laid his hand on her cheek in a rare gesture of complete gentleness. "That's a dangerous thing to tell me when we're alone."

She touched her hand to his briefly, then carefully drew it away from her skin. "I didn't intend to tell you at all. I don't think I realized it myself until you walked in here." Her sigh was both puzzled and wistful. "I just don't understand it."

"I wonder why it is we both feel we need to," he said half to himself.

Abruptly, she jumped up and began dropping what she thought she'd need into the tote bag. "I'm going to

the beach for snorkeling and sightseeing," Serena told
him. "Would you like to come with me?"

She didn't hear him move—he didn't make a sound
—but she knew he'd risen to stand behind her. For the
first time in a year Serena felt the light panic of
claustrophobia.

Justin placed his hands on her shoulders and turned
her to face him. Those eyes, he thought. That impossi-
bly rich color. It seemed he had only to look into them
for the need to spread to his. "A truce?" he asked.

She saw, with relief, that he wasn't going to press the
advantage she'd given him. "What fun would that be?"
Serena retorted. "You can come with me if you want,
but no truce."

"Those seem like reasonable terms," he mused.
When he slipped his hands around her waist, Serena
stuck the tote bag between them. Justin glanced at it,
then at her. "That's hardly an obstacle."

"The offer was for sightseeing," she reminded him.
"Take it or leave it."

"We'll go with that." With a hesitation so slight it
went unnoticed, Justin dropped his hands. "For now."

Accepting this, Serena turned and opened the door.
"Ever been on a glass-bottom boat?"

"No."

"You're going to love it," she promised, and reached
for his hand.

Her skin was wet and warm and glistening in the
sunlight. Two tiny scraps of material clung to the curves
of her breasts and hips. As she stretched out her legs on
the blanket, Serena gave a contented sigh.

"I like to think of the pirates." She looked out over the magnificent blue water and could almost see the Jolly Roger fluttering in the breeze. High green mountains rose around them, as if floating on the sea itself. "Three hundred years ago." Shaking back her wet hair, she smiled over at Justin. "Hardly any time at all, really, when you think of how long these islands have been here."

A few droplets of water glistened on his dark skin. "Don't you think Blackbeard might be a bit upset if he saw all this?" He gestured to indicate the people dotting the white sand beach and splashing in the turquoise water. Laughter rose with the scent of suntan lotion. "Unlike the rest of us, I don't think he'd consider these beaches unspoiled."

She laughed, both refreshed and exhilarated from their hour of snorkeling. "He'd find another place. Pirates have a knack for it."

"You sound as though you admire them."

"It's easy to romanticize after a couple of centuries." Serena leaned back on her elbows, enjoying the sensation of drying in the sun. "And I suppose I've always admired people who lived by their own rules."

"At any price?"

"Oh, you're going to be practical." Serena tilted her face toward the sun. The sky was as blue as the water, and cloudless. "It's too beautiful here to be practical. There's as much barbarism and cruelty today as there was three hundred years ago, and not nearly as much adventure. I'd love a ride in H. G. Wells's time machine."

Intrigued, Justin picked up the comb she had discarded and began to run it through her hair. "Where would you go?"

"Arthur's Britain, Plato's Greece, Caesar's Rome." She sighed, finding the sensation of Justin drawing the comb through her hair both sensual and soothing. "Hundreds of other places. I'd have to meet Rob Roy in Scotland or my father would never forgive me. I'd like to have seen the West before the settlers discovered it, but then, I suppose I'd've been on the first wagon to Oregon." Laughing, she tilted her head back farther so that she had an upside-down view of his face. "It would've been worth the risk of being scalped by your ancestors."

Justin weighed her hair in one hand. "It would have been quite a prize."

"I'd just as soon have kept it," Serena admitted wryly. "What about you?" she asked. "Wouldn't you like to go back a couple of centuries and play Red Dog in a Tombstone saloon?"

"They didn't welcome Comanches."

Reaching back, she brushed damp hair from his forehead. "You're being practical again."

His eyes held hers a moment. "I would have been in the war party, attacking your wagon train."

"Yes." She looked out to sea again. It was foolish to forget who and what he was, even for a moment. He was different. It only added to the attraction. "I suppose you would have. We would have been forging new frontiers, you would have been defending what was already yours. The lines get misted and you wonder if either side was wrong in the beginning. Do you ever feel cheated?" she wondered aloud. "Your birthright?"

Justin drew the comb slowly through her hair. As it dried he could see all the subtle shade variations that merged together for the rich gold. "I prefer making what I own rather than thinking of inheritances."

She nodded, because the words so exactly expressed her own feelings. "The MacGregors were persecuted in Scotland, forced to give up their name, their plaid, and their land. If I'd been there, I would have fought. Now it's just a fascinating story." She gave a low laugh as her mood shifted. "One my father will tell again and again at the least provocation."

A toddler, racing across the sand to escape her mother, landed like a plump ball in Serena's lap. Giggling, she tossed her arms around Serena's neck and clung as if they were in the conspiracy together.

"Well, hello." With a laugh Serena returned the hug, then she tilted the child's head back enough to see fun-filled brown eyes. "Making a break for it, are you?"

The girl grabbed a handful of Serena's hair. "Pretty."

"What a bright child," she commented, looking over her shoulder at Justin. To her surprise, he hoisted the child onto his own lap and touched a finger to her button nose. "You're pretty too." With another peal of giggles she pressed a wet kiss to his cheek.

Before Serena had gotten over her surprise at the ease with which he accepted the damp greeting, a woman in a trim black maillot rushed to the trio breathlessly. "Rosie!" The frazzled mother held a plastic pail and shovel while her cheeks grew pink. "Oh, I'm so sorry."

"Pretty," Rosie claimed again, giving Justin another kiss. This time Serena burst into giggles.

"Rosie!" Exasperated, the mother ran a hand through her hair. "I really am sorry," she repeated. "She heads everywhere at a dead run. No one's safe."

"When you run there's more time to play once you're there, isn't there, Rosie?" Serena stroked the warm brown hair as she smiled her reassurance at the mother. "She must keep you busy."

"Exhausted," the woman admitted. "But really, I—"

"Don't apologize." Gently Justin brushed the sand from the child's hand. "She's beautiful."

Obviously pleased, the mother relaxed, then held out her hand to her daughter. "Thank you. Do you have children?"

It took Serena a moment to realize they were being addressed as a couple. Before she could recover, Justin was already answering. "Not yet. I don't suppose this one's for sale."

Hefting Rosie on her hip, the young woman beamed down at him. "No, though there are times I'm tempted to rent her out. She's a handful. Thanks again. Not everyone appreciates being attacked by a two-year-old tornado. Say good-bye, Rosie."

"'Bye!" Rosie waved a chubby hand over her mother's shoulder before she made a valiant effort to scramble down again. Serena could hear her high, delighted giggles as the mother and daughter moved across the beach.

"Really, Justin." Serena brushed away the sand

Rosie had brought with her. "Why did you tell that woman we didn't have any children yet?"

"We don't."

"You know very well what I mean," she began.

"Now who's being practical?" Before Serena could retort, he wrapped his arms around her waist and pressed his lips to her shoulder. Instead of resisting, she leaned back against him a moment, enjoying the closeness.

"She was sweet."

"Most children are." He pressed a kiss to her other shoulder. "They've no pretensions, no prejudices, and very little fear. Soon her mother will teach her not to talk to strangers. Necessary, but rather sad."

Serena drew away so that she could turn around and look at him fully. "I wouldn't have believed you'd give children a moment's thought."

Justin started to tell her that the moment with the child that they had shared had awakened urges in him, a need for family he'd almost forgotten he had. A woman beside him, a child reaching up for a kiss. Then he brushed the thought away even as Serena brushed away sand. It was best to tread lightly on ground you didn't know, he thought. "I started out that way myself," he said at length.

She noticed his hesitation, but found her own emotions strangely muddled. "Are you sure?" Smiling, she rested her hands on his shoulders.

"Reasonably."

"I'm going to tell you something," Serena said solemnly, leaning a bit closer.

"Yes?"

"I don't think you're pretty."

"Children have a clearer outlook than adults."

"You don't even have a pretty nature," she insisted, but found the urge to press her lips to his too difficult to resist.

"Neither do you." Running his hands up her back, Justin deepened the kiss. His lids had lowered as hers had, but neither closed. She felt something creep out of her while her bones were softening, something small and vital that was hers one moment and his the next. Serena yielded to him in a kiss that held more promise than passion.

"I never intend to have one," she murmured.

"Thank God." His hand tightened in her hair suddenly, briefly, though his mouth remained gentle on hers.

Serena drew away. Something had changed. There was no clear explanation why, no idea what, but something had changed. There was a need to put things back on a solid footing until she had the time to decipher it. Her body felt soft and weak and alien.

"We'd better go," she managed. "I have some things to pick up in town before I'm due back at the ship."

" 'Time and tide wait for no man,' " he mused.

"That's about it." Rising, she shook loose sand from her romper before she slipped it over her suit.

"You won't always have that excuse." Justin stood beside her, halting the hands that worked her buttons.

"No," Serena agreed, then began to fasten the romper again. "But I have it now."

It took some artful driving through the traffic of

Charlotte Amalie, then a dash of luck to find an empty parking place. The streets were jammed with cabs, people, and small open-air busses with gaily patterned roofs. During this time both Justin and Serena were silent, occupied with their separate thoughts.

What had happened, she wondered, during that brief, almost friendly kiss on the beach? Why had it left her feeling like jelly inside, apprehensive and somehow delighted? Perhaps it had something to do with how touched she'd been to see Justin with the little girl. It was difficult to imagine a man like him, a gambler with those parallel streaks of coolness and ruthlessness, being a sucker for a twenty-pound brunette with sticky, salty hands. She simply hadn't given him credit for that quality of sweetness.

It could also be the fact that where she'd once thought she *might* like him, Serena now knew she *did*. But cautiously, she added, as if to reassure herself. It would never be wise to completely drop caution in any dealings with Justin. And now that she could admit she liked him and enjoyed his company, the cruise was almost over. During what was left of it, Serena would be kept so busy by her shifts and duties in the casino that she wouldn't have a leisurely hour to spend with him, much less a leisurely day. For the rest of the trip they would be at sea, with the casino open sixteen hours a day.

Of course there was still the option of accepting his job offer. Frowning slightly, Serena glanced out the window to see a table on the sidewalk near Gucci covered with hats made from palm leaves. For the past two days she had deliberately blocked the proposition out of her head—first from temper, then from the sensible notion that it would be better to consider it after there was some distance between them. Atlantic City would be an adventure. Working with Justin would be a risk. Perhaps one was the same as the other.

Why did the sudden softening of her attitude worry him? Justin wondered. That had, after all, been one of his goals. He wanted her, just as he had wanted her the first moment he had seen her. Yet, the days of contact, of arguments, laughter, and passion had added some new aspect to what should have remained a basic need.

It wasn't as simple as it had once been to attribute his conflicting emotions to the machinations of her father. In truth, he hadn't thought of her as Daniel MacGregor's daughter in days. As he pulled into an empty space, Justin decided it might be wise to think of her that way again . . . at least for the moment.

"More key chains that play *Für Elise*?" he asked as he switched off the ignition. Despite what he had just told himself, Justin drew her closer to taste her lips again.

"I never repeat myself," she retorted, but she didn't move away.

"Just this once," he murmured, "make an exception."

On a low laugh she increased the pressure until they both forgot they were in a parked car in the middle of a crowded city. Tonight, she thought, as her fingers ran up his cheek on their journey to his hair. The time had come to stop pretending and take what she wanted.

"Serena." It was half sigh, half moan as he drew her away.

"I know." For a moment she rested her head against his shoulder. "We seem destined to find ourselves in public places." She took a quick, audible breath and scooted out of the car. "Since we spent so long at the beach, I won't have time for anything but the most disciplined shopping." Justin walked around to her to take her hand. Serena smiled, then with a quick glance up and down the narrow, crowded street, she pointed. "I should be able to pick up a few souvenirs and the liquor I need in there."

Before she could reach her destination, the window display at Cartier's stopped her. Her long sigh was part appreciation and part desire. "Why is it an intelligent woman can find herself coveting a bunch of shiny rocks?" she wondered aloud.

"It's natural, isn't it?" Justin moved to stand beside her, letting his gaze roam over the sparkle of diamonds, the gleam of emeralds. "Most women are attracted to diamonds—most men too."

"Pressurized carbon," she mused, then sighed again. "Hunks of rock dug out of caves. Centuries ago we used them as amulets to ward off evil spirits or bring good luck. The Phoenicians traveled to the Baltic countries of Europe for amber. Wars have been fought over them, countries exploited . . . and somehow that makes them more attractive."

"Don't you ever indulge yourself?"

Serena turned away from the window and smiled at him. "No, it gives me something to look forward to. I've promised myself that the next time I travel it'll be strictly for relaxation. Then I'm going on a binge that may put a serious hole in my bank account. For now"—she gestured toward the next shop—"I need to pick up some more traditional sort of souvenirs for a few cousins, and a case of Chivas Regal."

Justin walked into the store with her, where Serena immediately became caught up in a flurry of picking, choosing, and buying. She generally disliked shopping, but once committed, did so with a vengeance. When Justin wandered off she paid little attention, engrossed as she was in a selection of embroidered table linen.

With the souvenirs purchased and wrapped, Serena went to the counter where bottles of liquor, liqueurs, and wines were displayed in profusion. A quick glance at her watch showed her she had nearly two hours before she was due on board. "A case of Chivas, twelve year."

"Two."

At Justin's voice, Serena turned her head. "Oh, I thought I'd lost you."

"Did you find what you wanted?"

"And more," she admitted with a grimace. "I'm going to hate myself when it comes time to pack." The clerk slid the two boxes of Scotch onto the counter. "I'd like mine delivered to the *Celebration*." Drawing out her credit card, she waited for the clerk to fill out the form.

"And mine," Justin added, counting out bills.

Serena pondered his case of Scotch while he relayed the necessary information. Strange, she mused, she hadn't thought him the kind of drinker to buy Scotch by the case. He never drank when he gambled. It had been one of the first things she'd noticed. Throughout the cruise, she'd seen him with a drink in his hand only once, during the picnic in Nassau. She decided perhaps he bought it in lieu of souvenirs, but it seemed odd he'd buy so much of one brand. After signing her name to the credit slip, Serena stuffed the receipt into her bag.

"I suppose that's it." Slipping her hand into his, she walked toward the exit. "Odd that we both bought the same brand of Scotch."

"Not when you consider we bought it for the same person," he returned mildly.

With a puzzled smile Serena looked up at him. "The same person?"

"Your father doesn't drink any other brand."

"How do you . . ." Confused, she shook her head. "Why would you buy my father a case of Scotch?"

"He asked me to." He guided her by a clutch of teenagers.

"Asked you to?" Hampered by another crowd of shoppers, Serena had to wait until she'd plowed her way through. "What do you mean he asked you to?"

"I've never known Daniel to do anything without a catch." Justin took her arm to guide her across the street as she was looking at him and not the cars. "A case of Scotch seemed reasonable at the time."

Daniel? Serena thought, noting the easy use of her father's name. For a moment her mind concentrated on that small point until unanswered and uncomfortable questions began to leak through. Disregarding the flow of pedestrian traffic, she stopped dead in the center of the sidewalk.

"Justin, you'd better tell me exactly what you're talking about."

"I'm talking about buying your father a case of Scotch for his thoughtfulness in booking my passage on the *Celebration*."

"You've got something mixed up. My father isn't a travel agent."

He laughed just as uproariously as he had the day he'd learned her last name. "No, Daniel's many things, but he's not a travel agent. Why don't we go down here and sit."

"I don't want to sit." She gave her arm a jerk as he led her to one of the cool courtyards. "I want to know why the hell my father would have anything to do with arranging your vacation."

"I think he had my life in mind, actually." Finding an empty table, Justin gave her a nudge into a chair. "And yours," he added as he sat.

She could smell the freshly made delicacies from the bakery across from them, hear the chatter from the little bookstore next door. Because she suddenly wanted to punch something, Serena folded her hands on the table. "What the hell are you talking about?"

"I met your father about ten years ago." Calmly, Justin drew out a cigar and lit it. Serena was reacting precisely the way he had expected. The predictability eased the tension he'd been fighting since that moment on the beach when he'd felt something slipping away from him. "I came to Hyannis Port with a business proposition," Justin began. "We played some poker and have been doing business off and on ever since. You've quite an interesting family." Serena made no comment, but her fingers clenched tighter.

"I've grown quite fond of them over the years," he

continued blandly. "You always seemed to be in school when I visited, but I heard quite a bit about . . . Rena. Alan admires your mind, Caine your right cross." Though her eyes smoldered, Justin couldn't prevent a small smile from curving his lips. "Your father nearly erected a monument when you graduated from Smith two years ahead of schedule."

Serena repressed the urge to swear, repressed the urge to scream. The man had been privy to her life for a decade without her knowledge or consent. "You've known," she began in a low, furious voice. "You've known who I was all this time, and you've said nothing. Played games when you only had to explain—"

"Wait a minute." As she started to rise he took her arm in a forceful grip. "I didn't know the blackjack dealer named Serena was Daniel's Rena MacGregor, the paragon I've heard about for the last ten years."

She flushed, both in fury and embarrassment. Most of her life she had found her father's bragging as amusing as it was endearing. Now it served as a cold, hard slap in the face. "I don't know what your game is—"

"*Daniel's* game," Justin interrupted again. "It wasn't until that day on the beach when you were shouting at me about MacGregors not being pushed around that I realized who you were and why Daniel had been so persuasive about my taking this trip."

Because she could remember the expression of utter shock on his face, Serena relaxed fractionally. "He sent you the tickets and didn't mention the fact that I worked on the *Celebration*?"

"What do you think?" Justin countered, tapping his

cigar in a plastic ashtray as he watched her. "When I found out your full name, I realized I'd been maneuvered by an expert." He grinned, amused all over again. "I'll admit it gave me a moment or two of discomfort."

"Discomfort," Serena repeated, unamused. Her brief telephone conversation with her father played back in her head. He'd been pumping her, she realized, wondering if his little scheme had borne fruit. "I'm going to murder him," she said quietly. Her eyes, dark with barely controlled fury, came back to Justin's. "As soon as I'm done with you." She gave herself a moment because the need to scream was building again. "You could've told me days ago."

"Could have," Justin agreed. "But as I figured your reaction would be essentially what it is, I chose not to."

"You chose," she said between her teeth. "My father chose. Oh, what marvelous egomaniacs you men are! Perhaps it didn't occur to you that I was on the chess board too." Anger flooded her face. "Did you think you'd get me into bed to pay him back for those moments of discomfort?"

"You know better than that." Justin spoke so mildly, Serena had to bite back a new retort. "For some reason I had a difficult time remembering whose daughter you were every time I put my hands on you."

"I'll tell you what I know," she said in the same dangerously low voice. "The two of you deserve each other. You're both arrogant, pompous, overbearing fools. What right do you have to intrude on my life this way?"

"Your father instigated the intrusion," Justin told

her evenly. "The rest was strictly personal. If you want to murder the old devil, it's your business, but don't stick your claws into me."

"I don't need your permission to murder him!" she tossed back, her voice rising enough to cause a few heads to turn.

"I think I just said that."

She sprang up, casting about futilely for something to throw at him. Since it was physically impossible for her to lift him and heave him bodily through the plate glass window of the bookstore, she only smoldered. "I'm afraid I lack your sense of humor," she managed after a moment. "I happen to think what my father did was insulting and demeaning." With as much dignity as she had left, Serena reached for her bags. "I'd appreciate it if you'd stay out of my way during the rest of the trip. I'm afraid I'd find it extremely difficult to restrain myself from throwing you overboard."

"All right. If—" Justin added before she could speak again, "you promise to let me know in two weeks about the position in Atlantic City." Even as her eyes widened and her mouth flew open to pour out abuse, he held up a hand. "Oh, no. Deal's off if you give me your answer now. Two weeks."

Stiffly, she nodded. "You'll get the same answer then, but I can postpone it. Good-bye, Justin."

"Serena." Smoldering, she turned back to glare at him. "Give Daniel my best before you murder him."

Chapter Six

$\mathcal{T}$he first thing Serena noticed during the drive from the airport were the trees. It had been some time since she'd seen oak and maple and pine touched with fall. It was barely September, but the feel of autumn was in the air, with all its strength and color. Even while she appreciated it, she seethed.

If it hadn't been indoctrinated into her to finish a job once it was started, she would have caught the first plane out of St. Thomas after Justin's relevation. Instead, she'd gone about her duties with an outward smile and inward rage. Rather than cooling off during the interim, Serena had grown more angry and frustrated, and felt more misused. Perhaps because Justin had kept his part of the bargain and steered clear of her for the remainder of the cruise, all of Serena's temper was fully focused on one man: Daniel MacGregor.

"Oh, you're going to be sorry," she muttered, causing the cabbie to glance quickly in his rearview mirror.

Nice-looking lady, he mused. Mad as a hornet. He began the gentle ride along Nantucket Sound in discreet silence.

The first view of the house had the effect of distracting Serena from plans of revenge. The gray stone glistened with minute pieces of mica in the late afternoon sun. It had been built to Daniel's fancy, and with its twin towers, as nearly resembled a castle as he could manage. There were large stone balconies, roughly carved, and tall, mullioned windows. A lush bed of flowers flowed in a semi-circle around the front—in place, Serena had always thought, of the moat he would have preferred.

From the main structure two lower stone buildings spread out. One was a ten-car garage, which with Alan and Caine away would be only half full. The other held a heated pool. Daniel might prefer a primitive style of architecture, but he appreciated comfort.

The cab pulled up in front of the granite steps, interrupting Serena's survey of the home she'd grown up in. Leaving the two suitcases and Scotch to the cab driver, she gathered together the sundry packages from her shopping sprees, and started up the steps.

Following an old habit, she looked at the massive oak door, where the MacGregor crest was carved into a brass knocker. Under the crowned lion's head was the Gaelic motto, which translated to "Royal Is My Race." As always, when reading it, she smiled. Her father had insisted they learn to say it in Gaelic, if they learned nothing else.

"Just set them there, thank you." Still smiling, Serena paid off the driver, then turned to thud her family crest against the door. It would reverberate through the house, she thought, like the sound of approaching cannon.

The door was swung open on its well-oiled hinges by a tiny scrap of a woman with iron-gray hair and pointed features. Her mouth fell open, accentuating the sharp chin. "Miss Rena!"

"Lily." Serena embraced the small, bony woman with all the exuberance of youth. In addition to her duties as housekeeper, Lily had been surrogate mother whenever Anna had been busy at the hospital. She had handled the three unruly children expertly, patching wounds and allowing squabbles to run their course. "Did you miss me?" Serena demanded, giving Lily a final squeeze before she drew the older woman away.

"Hardly noticed you were gone." Lily gave her a welcoming smile. "Where's your tan?"

"In my imagination."

"Lily, wasn't that the door?" Holding a piece of needlepoint in one hand, Anna MacGregor poked her head out of a doorway down the long hall. "Rena!" She came forward, her arms outstretched. Serena raced into them.

Anna was soft and strong. Both qualities flowed through Serena, along with a hundred memories. She took a deep breath, inhaling the scent of apple blossoms her mother had worn as long as she could remember.

"Welcome home, darling. We weren't expecting you until tomorrow."

"I caught an earlier plane." Serena pulled back, tilting her head so that she could study her mother's face. The skin was still creamy, with only a few fine lines betraying her age. There was a youthful softness about Anna's face that Serena thought she would never lose. Her eyes were calm, reflecting a nature that had refused to change through years of operating rooms and death. Her hair waved gently, a rich brown dashed with gray. "Mom." Serena pressed her cheek against her mother's again. "How do you stay so beautiful?"

"Your father insists on it."

Laughing, Serena pulled away, grasping one of her mother's strong, skilled hands. "It's good to be home."

"You look wonderful, Rena." Anna studied her with an easy mixture of maternal pride and professionalism. "Nothing better than moist sea air for the complexion. Lily, please tell Cook that Miss Rena's home; we'll have our welcome-home dinner a day early. I want you to tell me all about your travels," she continued, turning back to her daughter. "But if you don't go up to see your father first, I'll never hear the end of it."

Abruptly, Serena remembered her mission. Anna watched her eyes narrow, and recognizing the sign, lifted her brows. "Oh, I intend to go up and see him, all right."

"Anything you'd like to tell me about?"

"Afterward." Serena drew a deep breath. "He's going to require your medical attention when I'm through with him."

"I see." Knowing better than to question her daughter, Anna smiled quietly. "I'll be in the parlor then.

We'll have a nice long talk when you're finished yelling at your father."

"It won't take long," Serena muttered, and started up the wide, curved staircase.

At the first landing she glanced down the corridor to her left. This was where the family slept, with Serena's childhood room three doors down on the left. The wing was a maze of twists and turns and shadowy corners. She could remember her brother Caine hiding behind a three-foot-high urn, then jumping out and scaring her nearly to death.

Serena had chased him for nearly thirty minutes until her temper had been defeated by the sheer joy of the chase. He'd let her catch him eventually, on the east lawn, where he had tossed her to the ground to wrestle until she was weak with laughter. How old had she been? Serena wondered. Eight, nine? Caine would have been eleven or twelve. Suddenly, she missed him with a purely physical ache of kinship.

And Alan, she mused, continuing her climb. He'd always protected her in an offhanded way. Perhaps because he was six years her senior, they had never indulged in the hand-to-hand combat she and Caine had been prone to. As a boy Alan had been scrupulously honest, where Caine had used the truth to suit himself. Never lying, Serena remembered with a faint smile. Just evading masterfully. Yet, in his own way, Alan had always worked circumstances to his own favor. She decided it was a basic MacGregor trait. Glancing at the narrow stairway that led to the tower room, Serena vowed that there was one MacGregor who'd be sorry for it.

Daniel leaned back in his chair and listened to the precise, boring voice on the phone. Bankers, he thought maliciously. It was a curse to deal with them. Even owning controlling interest in the bank didn't protect him from them.

"Give them a thirty-day extension on the loan," he ordered finally. "Yes, I'm aware of the figures, you just gave me the figures." *Dunderhead,* he added to himself. Impatiently, he drummed his fingers on the desk. Why was it bankers couldn't see beyond two plus two? "Thirty days," he repeated. "With the standard penalty rate of interest." He heard the loud thump at his door and was about to bellow at the intruder when it swung open. Annoyance was immediately flooded by pleasure. "Do it," he barked into the phone before he slammed it down. "Rena!"

Before he could heave himself from his chair, she had advanced on him. Planting herself in front of the desk, she slapped her palms down on it and leaned over.

"You old goat."

Settling his bulk back in the chair, Daniel cleared his throat. The fat, he concluded, was in the fire. "You look well, too."

"How . . . dare . . . you." She spaced the words slowly and evenly—the next danger signal. "How dare you dangle me in front of Justin Blade like a piece of prime beef?"

"Beef?" Daniel gave her an incredulous look. Pretty girl, he thought proudly. A true MacGregor. "I don't know what you're talking about," he went on. "So, you met Justin Blade. Fine boy."

She made a sound deep in her throat. "You set me up. Hatching your little plot right here in this room like some mad king with a surplus daughter on his hands. Why didn't you just draw up a contract?" Serena demanded as her voice rose. "It's no less than I expect from you. Daniel Duncan MacGregor hereby trades his only daughter to Justin Blade for a case of twelve-year-old Scotch." She smacked her hand on the redwood. "You could even have put in provisions about the number of progeny you expected me to provide to carry on the family name. I'm surprised you didn't offer him a dowry!"

"Now, listen here, little girl—"

"Don't you little-girl me." She stalked around his desk and swung his chair around to face her. "It was despicable. I've never been so humilated in my life!"

"I don't know what you're talking about. I persuaded a friend to take a relaxing cruise."

"Don't you try to weasel out of it." She poked a slim finger into his massive chest. "You sent him on my ship hoping we'd trip over each other enough times so your investment would pay off."

"You might never have met him at all!" he thundered. "It's a big boat."

"Ship!" she thundered back. "It's a big ship and a small casino. You knew damn well the odds were in your favor."

"Well, what's the harm in that?" he wanted to know at the top of his lungs. "You met a young friend of mine. You've met hundreds of friends of mine."

The sound came from her throat again. This time

Serena whirled away. There was a huge bookshelf along the east wall. Stomping to it, Serena pulled out a volume titled *Constitutional Convention*. She flipped it open, revealing the hollow where six cigars were secreted. Watching her father, she scooped them out then broke them in half.

"Rena!" he said in quiet horror.

"It's the next best thing to poisoning you," she told him, dusting off her fingers.

Holding a hand to his heart, Daniel rose. His broad-featured face was wreathed in gloom. "It's a dark day when a daughter betrays her own father."

"Betrays!" she shouted, advancing on him again. "You have the nerve, the utter gall, to talk to me of betrayal?" Sticking her hands on her hips, she glared up at him. "I don't know how Justin feels about it, but I can tell you, I'm insulted by your little scheme."

He bristled, but noted her use of Justin's first name. Perhaps things were not as bad as they seemed. "That's the thanks I get for caring for my daughter's happiness. There's nothing sharper than the tongue of an ungrateful child."

"The butcher knife I was considering is."

"You said poison," he reminded her.

"I'm flexible." Then she smiled slowly. "Well, just so you won't think your money went for nothing, I suppose I should tell you what I've decided about Justin."

"Well, then . . ." Daniel went back to his desk, thinking she would be more reasonable now that she'd shouted and raged a bit. A pity about the cigars though.

"He's a fine boy, good brains, integrity, pride." He folded his hands over his stomach, prepared to be magnanimous and forgiving.

"Oh, yes, I quite agree," she said in dulcet tones. "He's also very, very attractive."

Daniel smiled, pleased. "I knew you were a sensible girl, Rena. I've had a strong feeling about you and Justin for some time."

"Then you'll be happy to know I've decided to become his mistress."

"I can't—" Daniel broke off, confused, then stunned, then outraged. *"The hell you are!* The day my daughter takes herself off to be—to be *kept* is the day I take a strap to her for the first time in her life! Aye, a strap, Serena MacGregor, grown woman or no."

"Ah, so I'm a grown woman now, am I?" While he blustered she gave him a long, hard look. "Remember this, a grown woman decides whom she'll marry, when she'll marry, and if she'll marry. A grown woman doesn't need her father arranging outrageously complicated blind dates. Just think about how this whole business could have blown up in your face before you stick your nose in next time."

Frowning, he studied her face. "You're not thinking of becoming his mistress then?"

Serena gave him a haughty look. "If I choose a lover, I'll choose one, but I won't be any man's mistress."

He felt a flash of pride along with a twinge of discomfort. It only took an instant for him to concentrate on the pride. Daniel pushed at a gold pen and pencil set on his desk. "Did you remember my Scotch?"

She tried to glare again, but the twinkle in his eyes undermined her. "What Scotch?"

"Aw, Rena."

Walking to him, Serena curled her arms around his neck. "I'm not forgiving you," she murmured. "I'm only pretending to forgive you. And I want you to know I never missed you at all." She pressed her lips to his cheek.

"Always were a disrespectful brat," he stated, hugging her fiercely.

When Serena went down to the parlor she found her mother sitting in her favorite rose-patterned armchair, working on her latest needlepoint project. On the rosewood tea tray beside her sat a dainty porcelain tea service dotted with tiny violets. Glancing at the scene, Serena marveled again that a woman who could be so happily domesticated on one level could be such a dedicated and brilliant surgeon. The hands that created the fragile pattern with needle and yarn would wield a scalpel on Monday.

"Oh, good." Anna glanced up as Serena entered. "I thought I had it timed well when I ordered the tea. Toss another log on the fire, dear, then come tell me about it."

As Serena moved to obey, Anna set her needlework on the piecrust table beside her. The fire was already crackling in the stone fireplace but roared at the addition of fresh wood. Serena watched the oak catch, then breathed deeply. Until that moment she hadn't realized how much she had missed the scent of burning wood.

"And a tub bath," she said aloud. Smiling, she turned to her mother. "Isn't it strange that just now I realize what an utter luxury it would be to soak in a bath for as long as I wanted? After twelve months of standing in a bucket that passed for a shower stall!"

"And you loved every minute of it."

Laughing, Serena sat on the hassock at Anna's feet. "You know me so well. It was hard work and great fun. But I'm glad to be home." She accepted the cup and saucer Anna passed her. "Mom, I know I'd never have met so many people, so many different kinds of people in my life if I hadn't done it."

"Your letters were always full of them. You should read them over yourself one day to bring it all back." Anna curled her legs under her and chuckled. "You'll never know how hard it was to talk your father out of taking an ocean cruise."

"When will he stop worrying?" Serena demanded.

"Never. It's part of the way he shows his love."

"I know." With a sigh Serena sipped her tea. "If he'd just relax and let me take care of my life my own way . . ."

"Why don't you tell me what you thought of Justin." When Serena glanced up sharply, Anna only smiled. "No, I hadn't the faintest idea what your father was up to. He knew better than to tell me. Your . . . ah, discussion with him was quite penetrating."

"Can you believe it!" Incensed all over again, Serena rose with the cup in her hand. "He actually duped Justin into that trip, hoping that I'd come home with stars in my eyes and orange blossoms in my brain. I've never been so furious, so *embarrassed*."

"How did Justin take it?"

Serena gave her mother a disdainful look. "I think he found the whole thing very amusing after his initial shock. He had no idea who I was until we were arguing on the beach one day and I said my full name."

Arguing on the beach, Anna mused. To conceal a smile, she sipped her tea. "I see. Your father thinks very highly of him, Rena. So do I. I suppose Daniel just couldn't resist the temptation."

"He's infuriating."

"Who?"

"Justin—both of them," she amended, setting down her cup with a snap. "He didn't tell me until the cruise was nearly over, and then in the most careless of ways. Why, I was actually beginning to . . ." Trailing off, she turned away to stare at the fire.

"Beginning to?" Anna prompted gently.

"He's very attractive," Serena muttered. "I suppose it has something to do with his unapologetic ruthlessness and that damned charm that sneaks up on you." Wisely, Anna remained silent, speculating. "Even when he made me furious he stirred things up inside me that would have been more comfortable left alone. I've never felt that kind of passion before. I'm not certain I ever wanted to." Turning back, she found her mother watching her calmly. "We spent the last day together in St. Thomas. I would have gone to bed with him that night—until he told me about Dad's little scheme."

"How do you feel now?"

Serena looked down at her hands, then let out a long breath. "I still want him. I don't know if it's any more than that. How could it be when we knew each other less than two weeks?"

"Rena, do you really trust your instincts so little?" Her brow creased, Serena looked back up at her mother. "Why should emotions require a certain time pattern? They're as individual as the people they belong to. When I met your father I thought he was a conceited, loud-mouthed ox." At Serena's appreciative chuckle, Anna grinned girlishly. "Of course he was. I fell for him anyway. Two months later we were living together, and within a year we were married." She made a wry smile at the obvious shock on her daughter's face. "Passion and premarital sex aren't the exclusive property of your generation, my love. Daniel wanted to get married; I was determined to finish medical school first. The only thing we both agreed on was that we couldn't, and wouldn't, live without each other."

Serena considered her mother's words while the fire snapped violently behind her. "How did you know it was love and not just desire?"

"Of all my children, you've always asked the most difficult questions." Leaning forward, Anna took her daughter's hands. "I'm not certain you can separate the two when it concerns a man and a woman. You can feel one without the other, but not when it's real love, not when it's real desire. Passion that comes quickly and then fades with time is only an echo. No substance, simply a result. Do you think you've fallen in love with Justin, or are you afraid you have?"

Serena opened her mouth, closed it, then tried again. "Both."

Anna gave Serena's hands a squeeze. "Don't tell your father; he'd be entirely too pleased with himself." This drew another reluctant laugh from Serena before Anna sat back again. "What do you intend to do about it?"

"I haven't thought about it. Rather, I've refused to think about it." She brought up her knees to rest her chin on them. "I suppose I've known all along that I'd have to see him again. He offered me a job."

"Oh?"

Serena moved her shoulders restlessly as ideas began to shift and sort in her mind. "Managing his casino in Atlantic City. It's a coincidence, because I'd decided to consult Dad about the possibility of opening my own gambling hotel."

"If Justin offered you a position like that, he must have a great deal of faith in your skill."

"I developed a knack for handling people," Serena mused as a thought focused.

"You developed it when you were two," her mother informed her.

"I've got a feel for the business," she went on with a hint of a smile on her lips. "I learned more than dealing cards this past year. In essence, the *Celebration* is one of the best run hotels I've ever seen, and though the casino's small-scale, all the basics are there. There wasn't any part of it I didn't learn from the inside out." She grew silent again as her smile widened. Anna recognized the look.

"What are you hatching, Rena?"

"I'm thinking of raising the bet," she answered. "Win, lose, or draw."

After tipping the bellboy, Justin stripped and headed for the shower. The maid could deal with the unpacking in the morning, and the casino could run another night without his attention. For now, he would have dinner in his suite while he made all the necessary phone calls to his other properties. With luck there would be no problems that couldn't be handled long distance. He had other things on his mind.

He adjusted the shower dial so that the water came out in pulsing jets. Serena would be home by this time, he reflected. And, if he knew her, Daniel would already be paying the price. Justin's grin came quickly, naturally. He'd have given a lot to have been within earshot during the reunion. It would almost make up for those last two long, boring, frustrating days aboard the *Celebration*.

Keeping his end of the bargain had been more difficult than Justin had imagined. To know she was within reach—dealing cards in the sophisticated tux, sleeping in that narrow bunk wearing only a flimsy handful of silk—had nearly driven him mad. But he'd stayed away because a deal was a deal—and because he had recognized that beneath her anger was a keen embarrassment that only time would lessen. The two weeks he'd given her should make her easier to negotiate with.

Even if she refused his offer, as he expected her to do initially, Justin didn't plan to leave it at that. He calculated he could taunt her to Atlantic City if necessary, and after she was there, he'd have house advantage. Flipping off the shower, he reached for a towel.

He needed a sharp manager downstairs. He needed a woman on the top floor. Serena was the only one who could fill both requirements. With the towel hooked around his waist, Justin walked into the bedroom.

Like the rest of the owner's suite, the room was spacious and sophisticated. The carpet beneath his bare feet was a thick, soft pewter. Long vertical blinds covered the glass doors to the balcony, and the touch of a button would swing them open, revealing a view of the Atlantic. He glanced at the wide bed covered in deep blue silk. How many women had slept in it? Justin neither knew nor cared. A night's mutual pleasure, they'd meant nothing more, nothing less.

From the closet he drew out a robe, letting the towel fall as he slipped into it. There had been years when he had lived in places smaller than this one single bedroom. He'd still had women. If he wanted one tonight, he had only to choose a number from his book and dial the phone. His body ached for one. Yet he knew that for the first time in his life just any woman wouldn't do.

Frustrated and restless, he roamed through the suite. He'd had good reason to base himself in the East. The Atlantic City operation was his newest, and the newest always required the most attention. It had never mattered to Justin where he lived. Over the years he'd grown used to the convenience of a hotel where his slightest wish would be seen to by the push of the right button. Now he found himself thinking about a home—something permanent, with grass to be tended and air that wasn't being shared with hundreds of other people.

Running a hand through his hair, Justin wondered why he should feel this vague dissatisfaction when he had everything he'd ever wanted. But his plans had never included wanting one woman. Was it because of her that he'd felt the lack of warmth when he'd entered his rooms again? If she were here, the echoing emptiness wouldn't be. She would fill it with temper and laughter. With passion.

Why had he given her two weeks? Justin asked himself angrily, stuffing his hands into the pockets of his robe. Why hadn't he badgered her into coming back with him, dragged her back so that he wouldn't be alone now, aching for her? He needed some contact with her—her voice over the phone. No, Justin thought more calmly, not her voice. That would only make matters more complicated. Going to the phone, he dialed Daniel MacGregor's private number.

"MacGregor."

"You old bastard," Justin said mildly.

"Ah, Justin." Daniel cast his eyes up at the ceiling, knowing he was in for his second tongue-lashing of the day. "How was your trip?"

"Educational. I take it Serena's already spoken to you?"

"Thrilled to be home," Daniel stated, glancing wistfully at the broken cigars on his desk. "Speaks very highly of you."

"I'll bet she does." With a grim smile Justin sat on the plump sofa. "Wouldn't it have been simpler to have told me Serena worked on the ship?"

"Would you have taken the trip?"

"No."

"There, then," Daniel stated reasonably. "And I'm sure it did you a world of good. You've been tense, boy, restless." He contemplated trying to light one of the mutilated cigars. "And don't worry, I'll talk to Rena for you, calm her down a bit."

"No, you won't. I'm holding a case of Scotch hostage, Daniel, until I'm certain you'll stay out of it."

"Now, now, there's no need to do that. It's just parental concern for both of you." These two certainly knew where to stick the needle, he mused glumly. "Why don't you extend your vacation a few more days, Justin, pay us a visit here."

"Serena's going to come to me," he answered flatly.

"Come to you?" The wide forehead creased. "What do you mean by that?"

"What I said."

"All right, boy." His chest expanded. "You'd better tell me what your intentions are."

"No." Some of the tension eased from Justin's muscles. Enjoying himself, he leaned back.

"What do you mean no?" Daniel roared. "I'm her father."

"You're not mine. You dealt me this hand, Daniel, I'm playing it out."

"Now, listen here—"

"No," Justin said again, just as calmly. "I'm telling you to fold, Daniel. Serena and I are going double or nothing."

"You hurt that girl and I'll skin you alive."

Justin laughed. "If ever there was a woman who could take care of herself, it's Serena MacGregor."

"Aye." Pride swelled his heart and distracted him. "The girl's a pistol."

"Of course, if you think she's going to make a fool out of herself . . ."

"No child of mine makes a fool of herself!" Daniel snapped, making Justin grin.

"Fine, then you'll keep out of it."

Daniel ground his teeth and scowled at the receiver.

"Your word, Daniel."

"All right, all right. I wash my hands of it, but the minute I hear that you've—"

"Good-bye, Daniel."

Justin hung up, satisfied that he had paid back his benefactor in spades.

Chapter Seven

Justin kept his office suite on the ground floor of the Comanche, connected by a private elevator to his penthouse rooms. He found the arrangement convenient, as his working hours were sporadic and there were times when he had no desire to pass through the public rooms of the hotel. The elevator was a practicality, as were the small television monitors in the far corners, and the two-way glass concealed behind the mahogany paneling on the side wall.

Because he demanded complete privacy in his offices, Justin worked in a large room without windows and with only one entrance. His experience in a cell had given him a long-standing aversion to closed-in places, so to compensate, he'd decorated his working area carefully. The furniture was light-colored—maize, oatmeal, biscuit—to give the appearance of airiness. The paintings were large and full of color. A desert scene caught in the last dying streaks of sun, the stark, unforgiving peaks of the Rockies, a Comanche brave in full gallop on a war pony. The color, and the lack of it, gave Justin an illusion of freedom that counteracted the restlessness he sometimes felt when he found himself trapped behind a desk.

At the moment he was reviewing a stockholders' report that would please anyone holding shares in Blade Enterprises. Twice Justin caught himself reading and retaining nothing, and forced himself to begin again. Serena's two weeks were up, and so, he discovered, was his patience. If she didn't phone within the next twenty-four hours, he'd be on his way to Hyannis Port to hold her to her end of the bargain.

Damn, he didn't want to go chasing after her, Justin thought as he tossed the report back onto the desk. He'd never chased after a woman in his life, and he'd already come uncomfortably close to doing so with Serena since the beginning. He played his best game when his opponent made the offensive moves.

Opponent, Justin mused. He'd rather think of her that way. It was safer. But no matter how he thought of her, he went on thinking of her. No matter what he struggled to concentrate on, she was always there, just at the back of his mind, waiting to slip through the guards. Every time he thought of having a woman, Serena was in his mind, almost close enough to touch, to smell. Desire for her completely obliterated desire for anyone else. Frustrated, hungry, Justin had told himself to wait her out. Now, he decided, he'd waited long enough. Before the night was over he would have her.

As Justin reached for the phone to arrange for transportation north, a knock sounded at his door. "Yes."

Warned by the tone in the one syllable, his secretary poked only her head through the doorway. "Sorry, Justin."

With an effort he directed his temper away from her. "What is it, Kate?"

"Telegram." She entered, a sleek, willowy brunette with a low-toned voice and sculptured features. "And Mr. Streeve's been hanging around outside. He wants you to extend his credit."

Justin took the telegram with a grunt. "What's he in for?"

"Five," she said, meaning five thousand.

As he tore open the envelope, Justin swore softly. "Jackass doesn't know when to quit. Who's on the floor?"

"Nero."

"Tell Nero Streeve's good for one more, then he's cut off. With luck he'll recoup a couple of thousand and be content with it."

"With his luck he'll be trying to trade his shares of AT&T for chips," Kate retorted. "Nothing worse than the spoiled rich who're temporarily short of fluid cash."

"We're not here to moralize," Justin reminded her. "Tell Nero to keep an eye on him."

"Okay." With a shrug Kate shut the door behind her.

Absently, Justin reached for the button that would

slide the paneling clear of the two-way mirror. It would be wise if he kept his eye on Streeve as well. Before he could press it, Justin's gaze fixed on the message line of the telegram.

Have considered your offer. Will arrive Thursday afternoon to discuss terms. Please arrange for suitable accommodations.

                                        S. MacGregor

Justin read the brief message twice before a smile tugged at his mouth. How like her, he thought. Short, to the point, and beautifully vague. And well timed, he added, leaning back. It was already past noon on Thursday. So, she was coming to discuss terms, he considered. Some small knot of tension unwound at the base of his neck. Drawing out a cigar, Justin lit it thoughtfully. Terms, he reflected. Yes, they'd discuss terms, keeping that area coolly business-like.

He'd meant everything he had said to her when he'd offered her the position. In his opinion, Serena was well qualified to handle his staff and his customers. He needed someone on the floor who could make independent decisions, leaving him free to travel to his other operations when it became necessary. With the rest of the hotels to oversee, he couldn't afford to spend all of his time supervising one casino. Blowing out a thin stream of smoke, Justin decided to make the job worth Serena's while. And once that was settled . . .

Once that was settled, he thought again, she'd have

to deal with him on a personal level. His eyes became opaque, his long, thin mouth set. This time there'd be no Daniel MacGregor playing the benevolent third party with an ace up his sleeve. Tonight he and Serena would begin a very private two-handed game. Justin's eyes cleared with a quick laugh. Winning was his business.

Picking up the phone, he punched the button for the front desk. "Front desk, Steve speaking. May I help you?"

"This is Blade."

The clerk automatically came to attention. "Yes, sir."

"A Miss MacGregor will be checking in this afternoon. Serena MacGregor. See that her bags are taken to the guest suite on my floor. She's to be brought directly to me."

"Yes, sir."

"Have the florist send some violets to her room."

"Yes, sir. A card?"

"No."

"I'll take care of it personally."

"Good." Satisfied, Justin hung up. Now all he had to do was wait. Picking up the stockholders' report again, he gave it his complete attention.

Serena handed the doorman her car keys and took her first long look at the Comanche. Justin hadn't gone for flashy or opulent, but had managed an excellent happy medium. The hotel was an open, V-shaped tower done in a drab adobe shade that brought a touch of the West to the East Coast. Serena approved the architecture, noting that nearly all the rooms had a view of the ocean. The drive circled around a two-level, grottolike pool with its own miniature waterfall. Coins glistened on the bottom. Obviously there were plenty who were willing to risk some loose change for good luck.

Beside the main door was a lifesize Comanche chieftain in full headdress. No dime-store Indian, Serena mused, but an exquisite sculpture in black-veined white marble. Giving in to the urge to touch it, she ran a fingertip down the smooth stone chest. How like Justin not to choose the ordinary, she thought as she let her eyes drift up to the marble face. Was it her imagination, or was there some resemblance there? If the eyes were green . . . Shaking her head, Serena turned away.

While her bags were being unloaded, she used the time to take a look at the boardwalk.

Famous names in huge letters on white billboards, bold neon signs, quiet in the late afternoon light, huge hotel after huge hotel, fountains, traffic, noise. But it wasn't the same as Vegas, she decided. And it was more than just the absence of mountains and the sound of the sea in her ears. There seemed to be more of a carnival flavor here. This was still a resort, she concluded, with a beach at the back door. One could smell the gambling, but it carried the moist salt spray of the Atlantic with it, and the laughter of children building sand castles.

Adjusting the strap of her shoulder bag, Serena followed her luggage inside. There was no red carpet or glistening chandeliers, but rather subtle mosaic tile and indirect lighting. Both surprised and pleased, Serena noticed huge leafy plants in pottery jugs and wall hangings that clearly depicted the life and culture of the Plains Indian. Justin's heritage was more a part of him than he realized, she thought as she wandered toward the registration desk. She could hear the familiar sound of slot machines muted by distance and the click of her own heels on the tile floor. Passing a bill to the doorman, she turned to the desk clerk.

"Serena MacGregor."

"Yes, Miss MacGregor." He gave her a quick welcoming smile. "Mr. Blade is expecting you. Take Miss MacGregor's bags to the guest suite in the penthouse," he told the bellhop, who was already hovering at her side. "Mr. Blade would like you to come right to his office, Miss MacGregor. I'll show you the way."

"Thank you." Nerves began to jump in her stomach, but Serena ignored them. She knew what she was going to do, and how she was going to do it. She'd had two weeks to work out her strategy. During the long drive from Massachusetts to New Jersey, she had gone over everything again and again. Once or twice she'd nearly given in to the urge to turn the car around and drive back north. She was taking an enormous risk with her future, and with her heart. Sooner or later she was going to be hurt. That was inevitable. But there was something she wanted in Atlantic City—and his name was Justin Blade.

She pressed her hand to her stomach once quickly, as if to push the nerves away as the desk clerk opened one of a pair of thick wooden doors marked Private. The brunette at an ebony desk glanced up in inquiry before her eyes rested on Serena.

"Miss MacGregor," the clerk announced.

"Yes, of course." Kate rose with a nod. "Thank you, Steve. Mr. Blade's expecting you, Miss MacGregor, just let me tell him you're here."

So this was why the boss had been on a short fuse, Kate concluded, giving Serena a cool, appraising look as she lifted the interoffice phone. She took in the long golden hair swept back at the temples with two ivory combs, the strong, elegant features accented by large violet eyes, the slim figure in a raw silk suit a few shades darker than her irises. Very classy, Kate decided, and as Serena met her stare without flinching, added—and no pushover.

"Miss MacGregor's here, Justin. Of course." She cradled the receiver, giving Serena a smile that stopped just short of friendly. "Right this way, Miss MacGregor." Leading the way, Kate opened another door. Serena paused beside her.

"Thank you, Miss . . ."

"Wallace," Kate responded automatically.

"Thank you, Miss Wallace." Serena took the door handle herself and gently closed it behind her. Kate stared at the knob a moment, realizing she had been expertly dismissed. More intrigued than annoyed, she went back to her desk.

"Serena." Justin leaned back in his chair. Why had he expected something to change? he wondered quickly. Somehow he had thought he'd be prepared for the onslaught of feeling simply seeing her brought to him.

Every hour of the past two weeks vanished in one instant.

"Hello, Justin." She prayed he wouldn't offer his hand, as her own palms were damp. "You have quite a place here."

"Sit down." He gestured to the chair in front of his desk. "Would you like something? Coffee?"

"No." With a polite smile she crossed the room to sit in a chair of buttery buckskin leather. "I appreciate your taking the time to see me right away."

He only lifted a brow at this. They'd circle each other for a while, he mused, like a pair of boxers studying defenses in the early rounds. "How was your flight?"

"I drove," she answered. "It was something I missed doing this past year. The weather was lovely," she added, determined to keep the trite conversation going until her nerves settled.

"And your family?"

"My parents are fine. I wasn't able to see Alan or Caine." Serena gave her first hint of a genuine smile. "My father sends his best."

"He's still among the living then?"

"I found more subtle ways of revenge." With grim pleasure Serena thought of the broken cigars.

"You're adjusting to land life?" Unable to resist the urge, Justin dropped his gaze to her mouth for a moment. It was untouched by lipstick and faintly moist.

"Yes, but not to unemployment." She could feel the brush of heat across her lips and the answering warmth that kindled in the pit of her stomach. She found herself wanting to go to him, to take whatever he would give on whatever terms he offered. Just to be held again, to have those lean, clever hands touch her. Carefully, she folded her own in her lap. "That's what I want to talk to you about."

"The position of casino manager's still open," he said easily, though he took his time bringing his eyes back to hers. "The hours are long, though I don't think you'll find them as all-consuming as on the ship. Generally, there's no need for you to be on the floor before five, though naturally you can adjust that from time to time if you need an evening off. There's a certain amount of paperwork, of course, but for the most part you'd be directing the staff and handling the customers. You'd have your own office on the other side of the reception area. When you're not needed on the floor, you can supervise from there. There are the monitors," he continued, gesturing. "And a more direct view."

Justin pressed a button, releasing the paneling. Serena glanced through the glass to watch the crowd in the casino, gambling, talking, wandering, in silent-movie effect. "You'll have an assistant," Justin went on. "He's competent, but not authorized to make independent decisions. A suite of rooms is included in your salary. When I'm away from the hotel you'll have complete authority in the casino . . . within my framework of rules."

"That seems clear enough." Unclenching her hands, Serena made herself relax. She gave Justin a mild, friendly smile. "I'd consider taking over the managerial duties of the casino, Justin . . . as your partner."

She saw a flicker, but only a flicker of surprise in his eyes before he leaned back. With anyone else it would have been a gesture of relaxation. With Justin it seemed a preparation for action. "My partner?"

"In the Atlantic City Comanche," she returned calmly.

"I need a manager for the casino, Serena; I don't need a partner."

"And I don't need a job, or a salary for that matter," she countered. "I'm fortunate enough to have financial independence, but I'm not of a nature to stay idle. I took the job on the *Celebration* as an experiment, I don't need to take another job for the same reasons. I'm looking for something I have a bit more of a stake in."

"You said once you were considering looking for work in a casino when you left the ship."

"No." She smiled again and shook her head. "You misunderstood me. I was thinking of opening my own place."

"Your own place?" With a quick laugh he relaxed again. "Do you have any idea just what that involves?"

Her chin came up. "I think I do. I've just spent a year of my life working and living on what was essentially a floating gambling resort. I know how a kitchen's run to accommodate over fifteen hundred people, how house-keeping keeps ahead of the linen supply, and how to stock a wine cellar. I know when a dealer's feeling under par and needs to be relieved and how to convince a customer to find another game before he gets nasty. There was little more for me to do on that ship than learn. And I learn very quickly."

Justin considered the coldly furious tone of her voice,

the hard, determined light in her eyes. She could probably do it successfully enough, he decided after a moment. She had the guts, the drive, and the bankroll. "Taking all of that into consideration," he began slowly, "why should I take you on as a partner?"

Rising, Serena walked over to the glass. "Do you see the dealer on table five?" she asked, tapping a finger against the window.

Curious, Justin rose and joined her. "Yes, why?"

"She has excellent hands—fast, steady. It looks to me as though she's worked out a very comfortable rhythm without appearing to rush the players along. She doesn't belong working midweek afternoons. You need dealers like that during the heavy traffic. The croupier at the crap table looks bored to death. He needs to be fired or given a raise."

"Clarify that one for me."

Because there was a touch of humor in his voice, Serena grinned up at him. "Given a raise if he takes the hint to be a bit more personable. Fired if he doesn't. Your casino staff should reflect the same attitude as the rest of the hotel staff."

"A good point," he admitted. "And a good reason for wanting you as my casino manager. It doesn't cover partnership."

Serena turned her back on the silent world behind the glass. "A few more reasons then. When you're needed out west, or in Europe, you'll know you're leaving someone in charge who has a vested interest— not only in the casino, but in the whole operation. I did a bit of research," she added. "If Blade Enterprises continues to grow at its current rate, you'll have to have someone help shoulder some of the responsibility. Unless, of course, you chose to work twenty-four hours a day making money without any time to enjoy your success. The money I'm willing to invest would give you enough fluid cash to sweeten your bid on that casino in Malta."

Justin's brow rose. "You have done your research," he commented dryly.

"We Scots never do business blindfolded." She gave him a satisfied smile. "The point is I have no intention of working *for* you or anyone else. For half interest I'll run the casino, *and* pick up the slack in other areas when necessary."

"Half," he murmured, narrowing his eyes.

"Equal partners, Justin." She met his eyes on level. "That's the only way you'll get me."

Silence came quickly and completely, and Serena forced herself to control her breathing to a slow, even rate. She wouldn't let him know how nervous she was or let herself think how easy it would be to forget pride and run into his arms. What had begun the last time they had been together had been quietly accomplished during their separation. She'd fallen in love with him when he hadn't even been around to tempt her. But he wouldn't know—she wouldn't allow him to know— until she was ready.

"Suppose you take some time to think it over," she said at length. "My plans are flexible," Serena went on as she walked to retrieve her purse from the chair. "I'd intended to look into some property here while I'm in town."

When Justin's fingers curled around her arm, Serena

made herself turn slowly. He was going to call her bluff, she was certain of it. And when he did, she'd have the choice of folding, or riding it out.

"Anytime during the first year that I decide it isn't working, I can buy you out."

She struggled against a shout of laughter. "Agreed," she told him quietly.

"I'll have my lawyer draw up a draft of an agreement. In the meantime you can get your feet wet in there." He jerked his head toward the casino. "You should have a week or so to change your mind."

"I have no intention of changing my mind, Justin. When I make a decision, I stick to it." Their eyes met again in a long, cautious stare. Serena held out her hand. "A deal then?"

Justin glanced at her hand, then slowly closed his over it. He held it, as though making a pact, then brought it to his lips. "A deal, Serena," he said. "Though we might both be sorry for it."

"I'll go up and change." She drew her hand away from his. "I'll work the casino tonight."

"Tomorrow's soon enough." Justin moved ahead of her to the door, closing his fingers over hers on the knob.

"I'd rather not waste time," she said simply. "If you could introduce me to my assistant and a few of the croupiers, I should manage from there."

"Whatever you want."

"Give me an hour to change and unpack then." Wanting to break contact, Serena twisted the knob.

"We have other things to talk about, Serena."

The words seemed to flutter along her skin. Aching

with need, she turned back to him. "Yes," she said quietly. "But I'd rather we cleared up the business preliminaries first, so it's clear one thing has nothing to do with the other."

Watching her, Justin caught the collar of her suit between his thumb and forefinger. "I'm not sure that one hasn't very much to do with the other," he murmured. "And that both of us aren't fools for pretending otherwise."

The pulse at the base of her throat began to hammer visibly. But even as he noted it, her voice came strong and clear. "We'll both find out soon enough, won't we?"

With a slow smile Justin dropped his hand. "Yes, we will. I'll see you in an hour."

It was going to be hard work, Serena discovered quickly. Every bit as hard as her work on the *Celebration*. But this time, she mused as she glanced around the crowded, noisy casino, she had her own stake. She signed her name to a cash receipt one of the croupiers brought her and felt a small glow of pleasure. Part of the life pulsing around her at that moment belonged to her.

Adjustments would take time, she reminded herself as she noted a few speculative glances aimed her way. When Justin had introduced her as his partner, Serena had almost heard the wheels turning inside each brain. She would simply have to prove herself qualified for the position no matter what happened between her and Justin personally. Rule number one was confidence. Rule number two was tenacity. When applied together,

Serena considered them an unbeatable combination—
not unlike the formula she used to handle her father.

Her assistant, Nero, was a big, quiet black man, who
had taken the news of Serena's interest in the hotel with
a silent shrug. She learned that he had worked in
Justin's first casino as a bouncer, and in one capacity or
another, had worked in all of Justin's properties. With
as few words as possible he took Serena through the
casino, gave her the basic routine, then left her alone.
He was one man, she concluded, who wouldn't be won
over easily.

Catching a signal from one of the dealers, Serena
crossed the room. Before she was halfway to the table,
she heard the angry raised voice. It took only a glance
to determine the man in question was very unlucky and
more than a little unhappy about it.

"Excuse me." Giving the players at the table a
general smile, Serena moved to stand beside the croupier. "Is there a problem?"

"You bet there is, sweetheart." The man on the end
leaned over and took her wrist. "Who are you?"

Serena allowed her eyes to lower to his hand, then
brought them slowly back to his face. "I'm the owner."

He gave a quick laugh before he drained his glass.
"I've seen the owner, lady. He doesn't look anything
like you."

"My partner," Serena informed him with an icy
smile. Out of the corner of her eye she caught Nero's
movement toward her, and imperceptibly shook her
head. "Is there something I can help you with?"

"I've dropped a bundle at this table tonight," he told
her. "My friends here'll vouch for that."

The other players ran the gamut between looking bored or annoyed. All of them ignored him.

"Would you care to cash in the rest of your chips?" she asked politely.

"I want a chance to make some back," he countered, setting down his empty glass. "This joker won't raise the limit."

Serena glanced at the poker-faced croupier and saw the dregs of fury in his eyes. "Our dealers aren't authorized to raise the table limit, Mr. . . . ?"

"Carson, Mick Carson, and I'd like to know what kind of operation this is where a man can't have a chance of getting even."

"As I said," Serena returned calmly, "the dealers aren't authorized to up the limit, but I am. How much did you have in mind, Mr. Carson?"

"That's more like it," he said, and signaled for another drink. Serena gave a small shake of her head to the roaming cocktail waitress. "Five thousand on the hand." He sent Serena a hard grin. "That should balance things out. I'll sign for it."

"All right. Bring Mr. Carson his tab, Nero," she ordered, sensing he stood within earshot. "You can play the single hand for five thousand, Mr. Carson." Serena shot him a level look. "And if you lose, you call it a night."

"All right, honey." He took her wrist again, letting his eyes travel down the length of the sleek ruby dress. "And if I win, why don't you and I go have a quiet drink somewhere?"

"Don't press your luck, Mr. Carson," Serena warned him with a smile on her face.

Chuckling, he took the clipboard Nero brought to him, then scrawled his name. "Never any harm in trying, honey. Oh, no," he added when Serena stepped aside. "You deal."

Without a word Serena took the croupier's place. It was then she caught sight of Justin standing to the side, watching her. *Damn!* She met his eyes briefly, wondering if she had let her annoyance get in the way of judgment. With another glance at Carson she told herself it would be worth the five thousand to get rid of him peacefully.

"Bets?" she asked, letting her eyes skim the other players as she counted out Carson's chips. By unanimous consent the others at the table abstained.

"Just you and me," Carson said, sliding his chips forward. "Deal."

Silently, Serena dealt him a seven and a two. A glance at her hole card revealed twelve with a nine showing.

"Hit," Carson ordered, reaching absently for his empty glass. She turned up a queen. "Stand," he said, and sent her a wide, mirthless smile.

"Stand on nineteen." Serena turned up her hole card. "Twelve . . . fifteen," she continued as she turned up a three. Without pausing she drew out a five. "Twenty." Carson let out his breath in an oath. "Come back again, Mr. Carson," she said coolly, and waited for him to stand.

He eyed her a moment as she calmly raked in his chips, then rising, walked out of the casino without a word.

"I apologize for the inconvenience." Serena smiled at the other players before she nodded to the dealer.

"You did that real smooth, Miss MacGregor," Nero mumbled as she walked passed him.

Stopping, Serena turned back. "Thank you, Nero. And it's Rena." She had the pleasure of seeing him flash her a smile before she walked to Justin. "Were you ready to have me committed?" she asked him quietly.

Justin looked down at her, then idly twirled the end of a lock of hair around his finger. "You know, I wanted you here for a variety of reasons. That was one of them."

Pleased, she laughed. "What if I'd lost?"

Justin shrugged. "Then you'd've lost. You'd still have handled a potentially uncomfortable situation with the minimal of fuss. And with style," he murmured, scanning her face. "I do admire your style, Serena MacGregor."

"Strange." She could feel the change inside her even as it happened—the softening, the heating. The wanting. "I've always admired yours."

"You're tired." Justin ran a thumb lightly under her eye, where the faintest of shadows was forming.

"A little," she admitted. "What time is it?"

"Around four."

"No wonder. The trouble with these places is that you lose track of day and night."

"You've already put in more than your share," he told her as he began to lead her through the casino. "What you need is some breakfast."

"Mmm."

"I take it that means you're hungry."

"I hadn't noticed, but since you mention it, I think I'm starving." Serena looked back over her shoulder as he nudged her through the doors of his outer office. "But isn't the restaurant the other way?"

"We'll have breakfast up in my suite."

"Oh, wait a minute." With another laugh she pulled up short. "I think the restaurant'll be a lot smarter."

Justin studied her a moment, then reached into his pocket.

"Oh, Justin—"

"Heads, my suite, tails the restaurant."

With lowered brows she held out her hand. "Let me see that coin." Taking it from him, Serena examined both sides. "All right, I'm too hungry to argue. Flip it."

With a deft movement of his thumb, he did. Serena waited until it lay on the back of his hand, then let out a sigh. "We'll take the elevator up," Justin said blandly.

Chapter Eight

"I'm still going to beat you one of these days," Serena said with a yawn as Justin pressed the button for the penthouse. "And when I do, it's going to be worth more than a breakfast." She glanced around at the smoky mirrored walls. "You know, I hardly noticed the elevator when I was in your office."

"It's an escape route," he said, then gave her a small smile when she looked at him. "We all need one occasionally."

"I don't suppose I thought you would." She remembered the two-way glass in his office and sighed. "Do they crowd you at times, Justin? All those people only a thin wall away?"

"More lately than they used to," he admitted. "I suppose you felt the same way on the boat occasionally.

Isn't that why you went out on deck when everyone else was asleep?"

She answered by lifting her shoulders. "Well, I'll have to get used to it if I'm going to be living here. In any case, I've always seemed to live in a crowd." When the doors slid open, Serena stepped through. "Justin, this is really lovely."

He used bolder colors in his personal rooms, slashes of indigo in the cushions of a low, spreading sofa, the flash of chartreuse in the shade of a glass lamp. For balance there were sketches in pastel chalks and a beveled mirror in a gilt frame.

"You can relax here," Serena decided, picking up a carved figure of a hawk in mid-dive. "It hardly seems like a hotel at all with your personal things around."

Oddly, when he saw her with her hands on what was his, Justin felt his first intimacy with the room. To him, it had always been a living arrangement, nothing more, nothing less. A place to go when he wasn't working. He had similar rooms in other hotels. They were comfortable, private and, he realized suddenly, empty. Until now.

"Of course, my suite is very nice," Serena went on, roaming at will to touch or examine whatever came to hand. "But I'll feel more settled in once I spread some of my own things around. I think I'll have my mother ship me my writing desk and a few other pieces." Turning, she found him watching her in the still, silent manner he could so easily slip into. Suddenly nervous, Serena set down a small glass bowl of cobalt blue.

"What sort of view do you have?" She moved toward the window, and had taken the first step up onto the small raised platform in front of it before she noticed that the glass table was already set. Lifting the cover from one of the plates, Serena saw a hearty Mexican omelet, a rasher of bacon, and a corn muffin. With a tilt of the lid on a silver serving pot, the aroma of fresh coffee filled the room. Beside the table was an ice bucket of champagne.

"Well, imagine that," Serena murmured as she slipped the single rosebud from its crystal vase. "Look what the good fairy left, Justin. Amazing!"

"And they say miracles are a thing of the past."

"You want to hear a miracle?" Serena asked him, passing the bud under her nose. "It's a miracle I don't dump this coffee over your head."

"I prefer to take it internally," he murmured as he crossed the room to join her. "Do you like your rose?"

"This is the second time you've made my eating arrangements before consulting me," she began.

"You were hungry last time too," he reminded her.

"That's not the point."

"What is?"

Serena took a deep, frustrated breath and was assaulted by the aroma of hot food. "I knew what it was a minute ago," she muttered. "How did you manage to have it here, all hot and ready?"

"I called room service before I came out to the casino to see if you needed rescuing." Draping a cloth over the bottle, he deftly removed the champagne cork.

"Very clever." Surrendering to hunger, Serena sat. Propping her elbows on the table, she set her chin on her folded hands. "Champagne for breakfast?"

"It's the best time for it." Justin filled two glasses before he joined her.

"*If* I decide to overlook your arrogance," Serena considered as she cut into the omelet, "this is really very nice of you—in an underhanded fashion."

"You're welcome," he murmured, lifting his glass.

After the first bite, Serena closed her eyes in silent appreciation. "And it's easy to overlook arrogance on an empty stomach. Either I'm starving, Justin, or this is the best omelet ever made."

"I'll give the chef your approval."

"Mmm. I'll have to take a look at the kitchen tomorrow, and the nightclub," she added over another mouthful. "I noticed you have Chuck Rosen for a week run. There shouldn't be an empty seat."

"I have him signed for an exclusive two-year contract." Justin broke a muffin in half. "He's a guaranteed sellout in all the hotels."

"That was a wise investment," Serena mused. "You know . . ." Lifting her wine, she studied him over the rim. "You're exactly what I thought you were when you sat down at my table the first time, and yet, you're nothing like I thought you were."

Sipping, Justin returned her gaze. "What did you think I was?"

"A professional gambler—which, of course, was accurate. But . . ." Serena trailed off and drank again. Justin was right, she mused. Champagne had never tasted better. "I didn't see you as a man who could build up and run a chain of places like this."

"No?" Amused, he toyed with his meal as he watched her. "What then?"

"I think I saw you as sort of a nomad. Which again is partially accurate because of your heritage, but I didn't consider you as a man who'd want the sort of responsibility hotels like these require. You're an interesting mix, Justin, of the ruthless and the responsible; the hard and"—she picked up the rosebud again—"the sweet."

"No one's ever accused me of being that before," Justin murmured as he filled her glass again.

"Of what?"

"Of being sweet."

"Well, it's not one of your dominating virtues," she mumbled into her wine. "I suppose that's why it throws me off when it comes through."

"It gives me pleasure to throw you off." His finger trailed down the back of her hand to her wrist. "I've found a certain . . . weakness for vulnerability."

Determinedly, she took another swallow of wine. "I'm not vulnerable as a rule."

"No," he agreed. "Perhaps that's why it's all the more rewarding that I can cause you to be. Your pulse jumps when I touch you here," he whispered, grazing a finger over the inside of her wrist.

A bit unsteadily, Serena set down her glass. "I should go."

But he rose with her, and now his fingers were laced with hers. His eyes, when hers met them, were very calm and very confident. "I made myself a promise this afternoon, Serena," he told her quietly. "That I'd make love with you before the night was over." Taking a step closer, Justin captured her other hand. "We still have an hour before sunrise."

It was what she wanted. Every pore of her body seemed to be crying out with need. Yet if his hands hadn't held hers so firmly, she would have backed away. "Justin, I won't deny that I want you, but I think it would be best if we gave it some more time."

"Reasonable," he agreed as he drew her into his arms. "Time's up." He stopped her protesting laugh with his lips.

There was no food to stop this hunger. His mouth was hard, devouring, before Serena could respond or struggle away. Yet she knew as he crushed her body to his that this time he would permit no struggle. She tasted his lips, and tasted urgency. She felt the firm, long lines of his body and felt need.

When his tongue sought hers there was no easy teasing, no gentle testing, but a desperate demand for intimacy. *Now*, he seemed to say to her. *There's no turning back*. What had begun weeks before with a long, cool meeting of eyes would reach its culmination. It would happen, Serena thought dizzily, because neither of them wanted any other answer.

Through those first urgent stirrings of passion she felt a quiet joy. She loved. And love, she realized, was the ultimate adventure. Placing her hands on either side of his face, she carefully drew her lips away from his, then looked into his eyes, warmer now with need for her. She wanted a moment, only a moment to clear her head, to say what she wanted to say without the heat of passion racing through her. Gently, she traced her fingers over the long, strong bones of his face. His heart thudded against her breast as hers began to calm. A smile touched the lips that were warm and aching from his.

"This," she told him quietly, "is what I want, what I choose."

Justin said nothing as he stared down at her. The simple words were more seducing than her soft summer scent, than the hot pulsing taste. They weakened him, exposing vulnerabilities he'd never considered. Suddenly, there was more than passion raging through him. Bringing his hand to hers, he slid it to his mouth, pressing his lips against the palm.

"I've thought of nothing but you for weeks," he said. "Wanted no one but you." He ran a hand down the length of her hair before his fingers closed over it in a fist. Need—good God, when had he ever felt such need? "Come to bed, Serena, I can't do without you any longer."

Her eyes were calm as she offered him her hand. Without words they walked to the bedroom. The room was in shadows, accented by the faint light that signals the end of night. And it was silent, so silent that Serena could hear her own breath as it began to quicken. When she felt Justin move away from her she stood resolute, suddenly tingling with nerves.

He wouldn't be gentle, she thought as she remembered the feel of his mouth and hands on her. As a lover he would be equally thrilling and terrifying. She heard a sharp scrape, then saw the flare of a match as he held it to the wick of a candle. The shadows danced.

Her eyes were drawn to him. In the flickering yellow light his face held a dangerous beauty. He seemed to belong more to his Indian ancestors now than to the world she understood. And she knew at that instant why the captive woman had fought against, then remained willingly with her captor.

"I want to see you," Justin murmured, reaching out to bring her into the candlelight. With surprise he felt the quiver run through her. Only moments before she had seemed so strong, so sure. "You're trembling."

"I know." She took a deep breath and exhaled quickly. "It's silly."

"No." He felt a streak of power, sharp and clean. Serena MacGregor wasn't a woman to tremble for any man. But for him, even as the fire lit in her eyes, her body shuddered. Taking her hair in his hand, Justin drew her head back. In the shifting light his eyes glistened with fierce, almost savage, desire. "No," he said again, then crushed her mouth to his.

She seemed to melt into him. Justin thought he could feel her bones soften, liquefy, until she was totally pliant in his arms. For the moment he would accept surrender, but soon he would have more, much more. With his mouth still avid on hers he began to undress her. Forgetting the fragile material, he tugged, pausing only to mold, inch by inch, the flesh he uncovered. She was shuddering now, pulling at the buttons of his shirt as her dress slid down to pool at her feet.

He'd known she would wear something soft and filmy. With a fingertip Justin nudged the thin straps of her camisole off her shoulders. But he didn't remove it—not yet. He wanted the pleasure of feeling silk between them. He tormented her, running hot, nibbling kisses over her face as she struggled to undress him. Her fingers touching his flesh wrenched a groan from him that he muffled against her throat.

Then she was beneath him on the bed, with only a fragile wisp of material separating them. He felt a madness, a driving need to take her swiftly that he had to fight back. Her breast was small and firm in his hand, straining against the silk as he rained kiss after savage kiss on her lips. Consumed by her, Justin drove her mercilessly to the first peak with only his hands and mouth. Swallowing her gasps, he pressed his body down on hers so that her frantic movements blended into him. Then ruthlessly, he slid down to capture her silk-clad breast in his mouth.

Struggling for air, Serena arched against him. Her body shuddered from a hundred unexpected sensations. She was trapped in a world of silk and fire. At her every movement, the bedspread caressed her naked back and legs, whispering of dark promises. Her flesh was seared wherever he had touched, as though he'd carried the tiny gold flame of the candle in his fingers. As he wet the silk above her straining nipple with his tongue, she felt the fire leap into her. Like a voice from a distance she heard him murmuring her name, and more she couldn't understand.

As if he'd lost patience with any barrier, Justin drew the chemise down to her waist so that he could feast on her naked skin. Serena pressed him closer, her hands now as demanding as his. Though her mouth ached for the taste of him, her body thrilled to the desperate race of his lips over her skin. She knew only pleasure now, the steamy pleasure of unrelenting passion. Gone were restrictions and rules; here was the abandonment she had glimpsed briefly in a dream.

It was only now that she realized there was so much she didn't know, so much she'd never felt. Second by second there were new discoveries. As his mouth tarried just above the line of silk, she felt a hunger deeper than any she'd ever experienced. Her imagination ran wild, thoughts of him inside her, filling her, dreams of a pleasure so acute they brought a tug of pain between her thighs. Delirious, she clutched at his shoulders.

"Take me," she demanded on a ragged breath. "Justin, take me now."

But he continued driving her higher, as if he hadn't heard her plea. He drew the silk down, caressing the newly exposed flesh with his lips—over the flat, quivering stomach, over the smooth curve of hip, to the taut, aching muscles of her inner thigh.

She arched, crying out, thrown swiftly into the river of passion. He was relentless, as terrifying a lover as she had feared, as thrilling as she'd dreamed. She was all that he wanted—soft and moist and out of control. Desperate, demanding, she clutched at him, scraping his flesh with those sleek, elegant nails. He could hear her moans, her incoherent words rasping out of her throat as he drove her further and further toward madness. Her skin was damp, beaded with passion, while her hips thrust her need toward him again and again. Now she was his, mindlessly his. And he knew, somehow, that no one had ever taken her more completely. Fighting to hold the power a moment longer, he ranged himself above her. Serena gripped his hips, urging him on.

In the first touch of daylight her face was like porcelain. Her eyes were closed, her lips parted as each breath trembled through them. Half crazed with need, he vowed no man would ever see her as he saw her at that moment.

"Look at me," Justin demanded in a voice harsh with passion. "Look at me, Serena."

She opened her eyes, and they were glazed with pleasure, dark with need.

"You're my woman." He slipped inside her and nearly lost control. "There'll be no going back for you now."

"Or for you." Her eyes lost focus as the two of them began to move together.

Justin struggled to comprehend what she had said, but she was moving faster. Burying his face in her hair, he swirled toward the madness.

Dawn streamed through the wide window in a flood of rose-gold light. With Justin's head still nestled at her throat, Serena watched it play over the length of his back. It looked like what she felt like, she discovered. Bright and rich and new. Was there a better way to watch the sunrise than with your lover's body warm on yours? Sleep . . . She felt no need for it. She knew she could lie like this for hours with the sun growing brighter and the sound of his breathing gentle in her ear. With a sigh sweetened by contentment, she ran her hands up his back.

At her touch Justin lifted his head. With their faces close he looked at her, letting his eyes roam feature by feature until there was nothing in his mind but her face, flushed and soft from loving. Without a word he lowered his mouth to hers in the butterfly touch he used so rarely. Gently, almost reverently, he brushed kisses over her eyelids, her temples, her cheeks, until Serena felt unexpected tears rise in her throat. Beneath his her body felt fluid and free.

"I thought I knew what it would be like," he whispered, touching his lips to hers again. "I should have realized with you, nothing's as I expect it." Raising his head again, he traced a fingertip under her eye. "You should sleep."

She smiled and brushed at the hair on his forehead. "I don't think I'll ever sleep again. I know I never want to miss another sunrise."

He kissed her lightly, then, rolling from her, brought her close to his side. "I want you with me, Serena."

Content, she snuggled closer. "I am with you."

"I want you to live with me," he corrected her, tilting her chin up so that he could see her eyes. "Here. It's not enough to know you're in a room down the hall." Then he paused, running his thumb over her lips. "There'll be talk downstairs, speculation."

Resting her head on his shoulder again, Serena began to trace a finger across his chest. "Talk won't stop downstairs once your name's linked with Daniel MacGregor's daughter," she told him.

"No." She heard the change in tone and knew that if she looked, his eyes would be unfathomable. "The press would find the relationship interesting, considering my background and reputation—as opposed to yours."

"Justin . . ." She trailed a finger down the center of his torso, then back up again. "Are you asking me to live with you or warning me not to?"

For a long moment he was silent while Serena continued to trace lazy patterns over his chest. "Both," he answered at length.

"I see. Well"—she turned her head so that she was free to nibble on his neck—"I suppose I should think about it." She felt a quiver of response as her hand ran low over his stomach. "Weigh the pros and cons," she continued, working kisses up his jawline. Shifting, she lay across him, her face just above his. "I don't suppose you could run through the pros again for me." With a smile she pressed her lips to his. "Just to refresh my memory."

"In the interest of helping you make an intelligent decision," he began, sliding a hand down to her hip.

"Mmm-hmm." But even as he sought to deepen the kiss, she moved, finding the vulnerable spot below his ear. "Did you know I was captain of the debate team my senior year at Smith?"

"No." His eyes shut as the heady sensation of being seduced took over.

"Give me a subject," she said, sliding her fingertips down his ribs, "and the time for . . . research," she added as she nipped gently at his throat. "And I can argue either side of the issue. Now, as I see it . . ." She gave a sigh of pleasure as she pressed her lips to the fast, jerky pulse at the base of his throat. "Living with you entails a great many inconveniences." His hand roamed over her hip, slipping between her thighs. Serena slid farther down his body, frustrating him.

"Serena—"

"No, I have the floor," she reminded him, then flicked her tongue over his chest. "I'd lose my privacy, and a great deal of sleep," she said, reveling in the quickening of his breath as she boldly explored his body. "I'd risk the inevitable gossip and speculation of my new employees as well as the press."

As muscles bunched and flowed under her hands, beneath her seeking lips, she lost her train of thought. Like the marble sculpture of the chieftain, she thought hazily as her blood began to pound. "You'd be impossible to live with," she concluded, lost somewhere between her own initiative and the savage beauty of his naked body. "Demanding, infuriating, and because I find you so incredibly attractive, I'd never have a moment's peace of mind."

She moved back up him, letting her body please itself by rubbing sinuously against his on the journey. Her smile was slow and seductive as she saw his eyes were fixed on her face. "Give me one good reason why I should, after considering all that, live with you."

His breathing wasn't steady, but he couldn't control it. The hand that grabbed her hair wasn't gentle, but he couldn't stop it either. "I want you."

Serena lowered her lips until they were an inch from his. "Show me," she demanded.

Even as her mouth came down to his, Justin was rolling her over roughly, beyond reason. He thrust into her quickly, wrenching a cry from her that turned to gasping moans as he drove her harder and faster. With mindless, grasping greed he took and took, but the hunger only seemed to feed upon itself, growing and swelling as her legs and arms tangled around him. He was drenched with sweat, trapped in those soft white limbs, unable to breathe, unable to break free. And it was her name that shouted over and over in his mind.

His body seemed to shake with the sound, threatening to explode with the desperate repetition of her name. Then the word shattered into tiny fragments. He knew he would never be rid of them, then he knew nothing but the shuddering relief of fulfillment.

Dazed, he slept, with his body and mind tangled with her.

The phone woke him barely four hours later. Beside him, Serena stirred, sighed, and mumbled an oath. Keeping one arm around her, Justin stretched out the other and plucked up the receiver.

"Yes?" Glancing down, he saw that Serena had opened heavy eyes to stare at him. He brushed the top of her head with his lips. "When?" Seeing him tense, she pushed up on her elbow. "Have they evacuated? No, I'll handle it. . . . I'll be down in a few minutes."

"What is it?"

Justin was already out of bed and heading for the closet. "Bomb threat in Vegas." He grabbed the first thing that came to hand—jeans and a cashmere sweater.

"Oh, God!" Serena was scrambling up, searching for her lingerie. "When?"

"The phone call said it would detonate at three thirty-five Vegas time unless we deliver a quarter of a

million in cash. That doesn't give us a hell of a lot of
time," he muttered, snapping his jeans. "They're still
evacuating."

"You're not going to pay." Fury in her eyes, Serena
pulled the chemise over her head.

Justin watched her in silence a moment, then smiled
—as cold and sharp as a knife. "I'm not going to pay."

As he strode into the next room, Serena dashed after
him. "I'll be down as soon as I change."

"There's nothing for you to do."

The elevator doors were already opening as she
grabbed his arm. "I'll be with you."

For an instant his features softened. "Hurry then,"
he told her, giving her a quick, hard kiss before he
stepped into the car.

In less than ten minutes Serena was rushing through
the reception area into Justin's office. He glanced up as
she entered, but gave her no more than a nod as he
continued talking in quiet tones into the phone. Kate
stood beside the desk, her hands clenched, her usually
composed face strained "Miss MacGregor." she said
curtly without taking her eyes from Justin.

"Could you fill me in, please?"

"Some nut claims he has a bomb rigged somewhere
in the Vegas hotel. He's supposed to have a remote
device that will set it off in"—she glanced at her
watch—"an hour and fifteen minutes. They're evacuating, and the bomb squad's sweeping the place,
but . . ."

"But?" Serena prompted.

"Do you have any idea how big that hotel is?" Kate

demanded in a shaking voice. "How small and deadly a bomb can be?"

Saying nothing, Serena walked to the bar at the far end of the room and poured a snifter of brandy. She brought it back to Kate, pushing it into her hands. "Drink this," she ordered.

With a shudder Kate tilted the snifter back until it was empty. "Thank you." She pressed her lips together a moment, then looked back at Serena. "I'm sorry. My husband lost an arm in Vietnam—a booby trap. This . . ." She let out a long breath. "This brings it all back."

"Come on, sit down," Serena said more gently as she urged her onto the sofa. "There's nothing to do now but wait."

"Justin's not going to pay," Kate murmured.

"No." Serena shot her a surprised look. "Do you think he should?"

Kate dragged a hand through her hair. "I'm not objective about things like this, but"—she brought her eyes to Serena's again—"he has so much to lose."

"He'd lose more than money if he paid." Turning, Serena ranged herself behind Justin. She touched him only once, briefly, a hand on his shoulder. As Kate looked on he reached up and caught Serena's fingers in his. The gesture told her more than a thousand words.

Why, he loves her, Kate thought, stunned. It had never occurred to her that Justin Blade would be vulnerable to a woman. Even as Kate studied his face, she wondered if he knew he was.

"He set off a charge in one of the basement storage

rooms." Justin let the phone drop to his shoulder a moment.

"Oh, God, was anyone hurt?"

He looked up at Serena with eyes that told nothing of his thoughts. "No. There's damage, but it's fairly minor. He called in to tell the police that one was just a bonus to prove he wasn't bluffing. He wants the money dropped off at three-fifteen, Vegas time."

Serena dropped a hand to his arm. "What are you thinking, Justin?"

"I'm thinking he's cutting it very fine for someone who's after a quarter of a million. I'm wondering if that's all he's after. When he called the hotel he asked for me by name."

Serena felt a new ripple of unease. "A lot of people know you own the Comanche," she began. "Or it's very likely someone who once worked for you, or knew someone that did."

He shifted the phone again. "We'll have to wait and see, won't we?" And there was something in the quiet words Serena recognized. A threat of violence, a promise of revenge. "How many more people left in there?" Justin demanded into the receiver. "No, I want to know the minute everybody's out."

"I'll get some coffee," Serena said.

"No." Rising, Kate shook her head. "I'll do it. You stay with him."

Serena looked at the trim gold clock on his desk. Ten forty-five. Moistening her lips, she gripped the back of Justin's chair and waited.

His eyes drifted to the clock as well. Less than an hour, he thought. And he was helpless. How could he explain that the hotel was more than concrete and stone to him? It had been the first thing he had owned, his first home after his parents had died. It symbolized his independence, his success, his heritage. Now he could only stand by and wait for it to be blown apart.

Was that the reason for the feeling in his gut that the threat was directed at him personally? Running a hand over the back of his neck, Justin decided that made more sense—and yet his instincts told him differently.

"It might be a bluff." Serena's voice came calm and strong from behind him. Justin felt the sharp wave of frustration pass. Holding out a hand, he waited for her to come around the chair and slip hers into it.

"I don't think so."

She pressed his hand between both of hers. "It would be wrong to pay. You're doing the right thing, Justin."

"It's the only thing I know how to do." He gave his attention to the voice over the phone. "Good. The guests and staff are out," he told Serena.

She sat on the arm of his chair while they both watched the clock.

Kate came back with coffee, but it sat untouched on the desk while they waited. As the minutes ticked by, Serena could feel the tension coming off Justin in waves. He sat silently, the phone in one hand. She tried to imagine the complexity of a search in a hotel the size of Justin's Vegas Comanche. How many hundreds of rooms, Serena wondered, how many thousands of closets and corners? She wondered helplessly if the sound of the explosion would carry through the receiver. And how many other times, she thought, has Justin's fate rested on the caprices of luck? This time, she told herself as she placed her hand back on his shoulder, fate would have to beat them both.

Because she was watching them, Serena saw the sudden rigidity in the fingers that lay on the desk.

"Yes."

To keep herself from asking questions, Serena bit her lip as Justin listened to the voice over the phone.

"I see. No, not that I'm aware of. Yes, I'll be there as soon as possible. Thank you." Hanging up the phone, he turned to Serena. "They found it."

"Oh, thank God." She dropped her forehead onto his.

"From what I was just told, it would have taken out the casino and half the main floor. Kate, book me on the first flight to Vegas."

"Justin." Serena stood from the arm of his chair and found her legs were oddly weak. "Do they have any idea who?"

"No." For the first time he noticed the coffee mug on his desk. Lifting it, he drank half of it down. "I have to go out, smooth over things in the hotel and talk to the authorities. I'll be back in a couple of days." He rose and took her by the shoulders. "It looks like my new partner's going to have a trial by fire."

"I'll be fine." Rising on her toes, she brushed a kiss over his mouth. "And I'll take good care of our hotel."

"I'm sure you will," he said, then drew her closer. "I don't like leaving you just now."

"I'll be here when you get back." She reached up to frame his face with her hands. "Don't worry, just come back soon."

He lowered his mouth to hers and lingered. "Go get some sleep," he suggested.

"Oh, no, this is my first full day on the job." His face was calm, but she could feel the tension in him. Instead of the endless questions she wanted to ask, Serena made herself smile and pull away. "I have quite a few things to do—tour the hotel, inspect the kitchen, go through the files in my office, arrange to have my things moved to our suite."

The *our* hit him forcibly, leaving him a little stunned. "Do that first," he demanded, taking her hands again. "I want to know you're in my bed. Serena, I—"

"You're on a plane in forty-five minutes, Justin," Kate interrupted, poking her head in the doorway. "You'll have to hurry if you want to make it."

"All right, have a car brought around."

"Justin." With a half laugh Serena tugged on her hands. "You're breaking my fingers." There was something in the look he gave her—part wary, part stormy—that had her smile fading. "What is it?"

Had he been going to tell her he loved her? he thought with a quick flutter of panic. Had he been going to say the words before they had fully registered in his mind? "It'll keep," he said at length.

"All right." And because she wanted to erase the tension from his face, she smiled again. Then, throwing her arms around his neck, Serena pressed her mouth to his. "Be miserable without me, please."

"I'll do my best. Kate has the number if you need me."

"Justin, your car's here."

"Yes, all right." He gave Serena a last, bruising kiss. "Think of me," he ordered before he strode away.

Taking a deep breath, she sat in the chair, still warm from him. "Do I have any choice?" she wondered aloud.

Chapter Nine

Over the next week Serena immersed herself in the routine of the Comanche. It was, she decided, her first major investment that hadn't been carefully chosen by her father, and one she was determined to understand intimately. She didn't mind a few speculative looks, the occasional murmured word behind a hand as she inspected the public rooms or pored over the books and files and records. She expected them. She spent her days learning the hotel from top to bottom, her evenings in the casino or her office in the capacity as manager. The nights she spent alone in Justin's suite.

Over the week she discovered two things. The Comanche was a slickly run organization that catered to people who had money to spend. It gave its clientele the best—for a price. And second, Justin's absence was a blessing in disguise.

She had little time to miss him with her hours packed with things to do. Only late at night when she found herself alone did Serena fully realize how much she'd grown to depend on him. For a word, a touch, his presence. But alone, she had the opportunity to prove to herself and to her staff that she was both competent and serious about running the hotel. Serena made the most of it.

Her background served her well. Over the years she'd become accustomed to patronizing fine hotels, and knew what a client looked for from check-in to check-out. Her year on the *Celebration* had given her another perspective. She understood the problems that plagued the staff—from fatigue to boredom to a shortage in the linen count. The first day she had won over Nero and Kate. By the second, Serena had swayed the chef, the night manager, and the housekeeper. She considered each one a major victory.

Behind the trim pecan desk in her office Serena went over the current week's schedule of her croupiers. Directly in front of her the panel was open, giving her a broad view of the casino. She found she enjoyed the twin feelings of isolation and companionship. Since the day had barely started by casino standards, she planned to give her paperwork another two hours, knowing if she were needed, the buzzer on her desk would sound, lighting up the location of the trouble. Then she'd work the floor. If she kept busy until weariness took over, she wouldn't be tempted to pick up the phone and dial Justin's number in Vegas.

He was a man who needed room, who didn't make promises or expect them. If she were to win in the end,

Serena knew she couldn't forget that. If she were patient, there might come a time when he'd be comfortable loving her. With a quick laugh she shook her head. She'd never be *comfortable* loving him. Nor did she choose to be.

Rubbing the back of her neck, Serena frowned down at the schedule. It could be made less complicated, she mused, if they hired one more croupier as a floater. That would make the hours a bit more flexible and . . .

"Yes, come in." Without glancing up, Serena continued to look over the list. With a floater to pick up the slack, she mused, she could juggle the shifts. Then suddenly a spray of violets landed on the paper in front of her.

"I thought that might get your attention."

Feeling her heartbeat speed, Serena looked up. "Justin!" She was out of her chair and racing into his arms before either of them expected it.

As his mouth came down to hers, he realized it was the first time he'd seen that spontaneous, unrestricted joy on her face. And it was for him. The fatigue of a long flight, the tension of a week, melted from him. "What is it about a woman," he asked her, "that makes it so good to hold one?"

Smiling, she tilted her head back. The closer study of his face brought concern. "You look tired." Her fingers rose to smooth away the lines of strain around his mouth. "I've never seen you look tired before. Was it very bad?"

"I've spent more pleasant weeks." He drew her back to him, wanting to fill himself with the feel of her, the scent. Later, he thought, he'd tell her of the neatly printed note he'd received. Another threat, without details or reasons, just a promise that it wasn't over. "I did what you asked," he added, running a hand over the smooth flesh the low back of her dress exposed.

"Mmm. What?"

"I was miserable without you."

She didn't laugh as he had expected, but tightened her arms around his neck. Fighting back tears, she pressed her lips to his throat. "You didn't call. I waited for you to call," she whispered. Appalled by her words, Serena pushed out of his arms, swallowing tears and shaking her head. "No, I didn't mean that the way it sounded. I know you were busy." She lifted her hands, then helplessly let them fall. "And—and so was I. There were a million things . . ." She turned to shuffle papers on her desk. "We're both adults, and independent. The last thing we need is to start putting chains on each other."

"You ramble when you're nervous," Justin commented.

Whirling, Serena glared at him with hot, furious eyes. "Don't you dare make fun of me."

"Odd that I would have missed that killing look," he said as he came to her. Taking her face in his hands, he held it gently, his eyes on hers. Serena felt her anger drain to leave her weak and pulsing. "Serena," he said on a sigh as his mouth closed over hers.

The tender kiss grew hungry quickly. She felt the need pour out of him to match her own as their lips clung, parting only to seek new angles, deeper pleasures. Longings of a week intensified so that there were two pairs of hot, avid lips searching, two pairs of urgent hands roaming. On a jerky breath Justin crushed her against him. No woman, he thought dimly, had ever made him suffer like this.

"Oh, God, I want you, Serena. I want you so that I can't think of anything but having you."

She pressed her cheek against his, but the movements behind the glass caught her eye. "This is silly," she admitted, "but I feel . . . exposed." On a shaky laugh she drew back, but the look in his eyes had her heart thudding again. "Why don't you close the panel," she whispered, "and make love to me." The knock on the door brought a groan from her.

On a long breath Justin drew her away until he held her lightly by the shoulders. "I forgot. I brought you a present."

"Tell them to go away," Serena suggested. "And give it to me later." She brought her hands to his. "Much later."

The knock came again. "Come on, Justin, you've had your ten minutes."

"Caine?" Justin watched surprise and pleasure race across Serena's face. "Caine."

Kissing her nose, he let his hands drop away from her. "Why don't you go let them in?"

Dashing to the door, Serena wrenched it open. "Caine! Alan!" With a whoop of laughter she launched herself at both of them. "What are you doing here?" she demanded, kissing them both. "Won't the state and federal governments collapse?"

"Even public servants need a few days off now and then," Caine retorted, then held Serena at arm's length.

He'd changed so little, she thought. Though both her brothers had inherited their father's height, Caine was lean and rangy. Nearly thin, Serena mused now with sisterly objectivity. Yet he had a fascinating face, all planes and angles, with a powerful grin he used to his advantage and eyes nearly as dark as her own. His hair waved carelessly around his face— blond with hints of red. Looking at him, she could easily see why it was reputed his skill with women equaled his skill as a lawyer.

"Hmmm. She hasn't turned out too badly, has she, Alan?"

With an arched brow Serena turned to her oldest brother. "No," he answered, giving her the slow, serious smile that suited his dark, brooding looks. He looks more like Heathcliff, she thought, than a U.S. senator. "Though she's still a bit scrawny." He took her chin in his fingers, turning her face right and left. "Pretty girl," he stated in a perfect imitation of their father's burr.

"Maybe you should have married Arlene Judson after all," she said sweetly. Then, relenting, she wrapped an arm around each of her brothers. "Oh, I'm so glad to see you!"

Justin sat on the corner of Serena's desk and watched them. She looked very small between the two tall men, but for the first time, he noted the resemblance between her and Caine—the shape of the mouth, the nose, the eyes. Alan was a larger, rougher version of Anna, yet all three of them carried Daniel's stamp. It seemed so clear now, Justin wondered that he hadn't recognized it the first moment he'd seen her.

Perhaps it was seeing them as a family, picturing Serena as a sister. He thought of Diana and felt a twinge of regret. He'd done all he could there, Justin reminded himself. Still, he'd never know what it was like to have that basic, lifetime kinship any more than he'd ever have the place in Serena's heart that belonged to family.

"How long are you staying?" Serena demanded as she pulled them both inside the office.

"Just over the weekend," Alan told her as Caine took a quick, thorough study of her office.

"So you've taken yourself a partner after all," he said to Justin. "We were all a bit surprised after you'd turned Dad down so often."

"I was more persuasive," Serena said simply.

Caine shot Justin a look that didn't ask questions only because he already knew the answers. There was warning in it, subtle, but perfectly clear.

"You still haven't told me what you're doing here like this." She walked over to stand beside Justin as Caine folded himself into a chair and Alan moved to glance through the glass.

"We heard about the bomb threat in Vegas," Alan told her. "I gave Justin a call. He suggested you might enjoy a visit. And"—he turned with one of his rare grins—"Caine and I thought our coming might keep Dad from putting in an appearance for a while."

"Last time I talked to him," Caine said, "he was hinting he might enjoy a few weeks at the beach."

Serena made a sound that was somewhere between a groan and a laugh. "I suppose you heard about his last little plot."

"It seems to have worked out well enough," Alan stated as he watched Justin's hand come up to rest on the back of her neck.

"I was tempted to break more than a few cigars," she muttered, then glanced down at the buzzer on her desk as it sounded. "Table six. No," she said, touching Justin's shoulder as he started to rise. "I'll take care of it. Why don't the three of you go upstairs and relax? I'll be up as soon as I'm sure everything is settled down here."

"Is it unethical for me to gamble here now that you're half owner?" Caine wondered aloud.

"Not as long as you play as poorly as usual," Serena answered as she swept out of the door.

With a quick oath Caine stretched out his long legs. "Just because I used to let her beat me at poker."

"Let her win, hell," Alan said mildly. "She used to massacre you. You didn't say much on the phone, Justin," he continued as he turned away from the two-way mirror. "Can you discuss what happened in Vegas?"

With a shrug Justin drew a cigar out of his pocket. "It was a homemade bomb, very compact. It was under one of the keno tables. The F.B.I.'s running down the list of former employees, regulars who've dropped large amounts of money, any known extortionists with a similar M.O. I don't have too much faith in that. There were some threatening calls, but they couldn't trace them and I didn't recognize the voice. They don't have much to go on." As he lit the cigar his gaze wandered past Alan's shoulder to where Serena stood, talking to a customer. "It's impossible to trace everyone who's lost money in one of my casinos, even if that is the motive behind the bombing."

"You don't think it was?" Caine asked, and followed Justin's gaze out to his sister.

"Just a hunch," he muttered, then rose restlessly. "There was a threat delivered a couple of days ago—nothing specific, just enough to let me know he'd try something else."

"No wheres, whens, or hows?" Caine put in.

"No." Justin gave him a grim smile. "Of course I could close down all of my hotels and wait him out." He took a quick savage drag on the cigar. "I'm damned if I will." With an effort he controlled the impotent fury. He was being stalked. He knew it just as surely as if he'd seen the shadow behind him. "I want Serena to go home until this is resolved," he said briefly. "Between the two of you you should be able to convince her."

Caine's answer was a short laugh. Alan gave Justin a quiet look. "She'd go," he said, "if you went with her."

"Damn it, Alan, I'm not going to go find a convenient hole and hide while someone plays with my life."

"And Serena would?" he countered.

"She has a half interest in one out of five of my hotels," Justin said tightly. "If anything happens to this one, the insurance covers her losses." His eyes were drawn to the glass again. "I've more than an investment at stake."

"You're a fool if you think that's all Rena has," Alan murmured.

Justin whirled on him, giving way to all the pent-up anger he'd harnessed for a week. "I tell you, I have a bad feeling about this. Someone's after me, and she's too close. I want her away, safe, where nothing can happen to her. I'd think you'd understand that. For God's sake, she's your sister!"

"And what is she to you?" Caine asked softly.

Furious, Justin turned on him, a hundred curses trembling on his lips. He met the dark, direct eyes, so much like Serena's. "Everything," he breathed before he turned back to the glass. "Damn it, she's everything."

"Well, that's settled," Serena said as she swirled back into the office. "I just . . ." She trailed off as the tension rose up like a wall. Slowly, she looked from one man to the other, then walked by her brothers to Justin. "What is it?"

"Nothing." Forcing himself to be calm, he tapped out his cigar and took her hand. "Have you had dinner?"

"No, but—"

Deliberately, he looked past her to Alan and Caine. "We'll have something brought upstairs, unless you'd prefer the dining room."

"Actually, I think I'll try my luck outside." Caine rose casually. "Alan can keep me from dropping a month's pay. Got any tips, Rena?"

"Stick to the quarter slots," she said, and made her lips curve.

"O ye of little faith," he muttered, and tugged on her ear. "We'll see you tomorrow."

"Late tomorrow," Alan put in as he opened the door. "I'll never get him away from the tables before three."

Serena waited until the door shut behind them. "Justin, what's going on?"

"I'm tired," he said, taking her arm. "Let's go upstairs."

"Justin, I'm not a fool." He led her quickly through to his office and into the elevator. "It felt like something was about to explode when I walked in there. Are you angry with Alan and Caine?"

"No. It's nothing that concerns you."

The cold, flat answer had her stiffening in defense. "Justin, I'm not trying to pry into your personal business, but as it appeared to involve my brothers, I feel entitled to an explanation."

He recognized the hurt, and the anger. He wanted to drive them both away, drag her into his arms and stop her questions in a way that would erase his own temper and tension. But as the elevator doors slid open, Justin forced himself to think coolly. He could use the anger and hurt for his own ends.

"It's nothing that concerns you," he repeated carelessly. "Why don't you order something from room service. I want a shower." Without waiting for her answer he strode off.

Too stunned by his tone to react, Serena only stared after him. What had changed since that desperate, tempestuous greeting they had shared? Why was he treating her like a stranger? Or worse, she realized, like a comfortable mistress a man could take or brush aside at his whim. Standing in the center of the room, Serena tried to summon up fury but found only anguish. She'd known the risk she was taking. It seemed she'd lost the gamble.

No. Bunching her hands into fists, she shook her head. No, she wasn't so easily dismissed. Let him have his shower and his meal, she decided. Then she would . . . *explain* to him exactly what she expected. Calmly, she added to herself as she walked to the phone. She'd be very calm. With a vicious stab of her finger she punched the button for room service.

"This is Ms. MacGregor. I'd like a steak and salad."

"Of course, Ms. MacGregor. How would you like your steak?"

"Burnt," she muttered.

"Pardon?"

With an effort she got herself under control. "It's for Mr. Blade," she explained. "I'm sure you know what he likes."

"Of course, Ms. MacGregor. I'll have his dinner sent up right away."

"Thank you." Everyone jumps for Justin Blade, she thought grimly as she replaced the receiver. Walking to the bar, she fixed herself a tall, stiff drink.

When Justin came out of the bedroom Serena was sitting on the sofa while the room service waiter arranged Justin's meal on the table across the room. Justin wore only a robe, which parted at the throat when he dipped his hands into his pockets. "Aren't you eating?" he asked with a nod toward the single place setting.

"No." She sipped her drink. "You go right ahead." Opening her purse, she drew out a bill, then held it out to the waiter. "Thank you."

"Thank you, Ms. MacGregor. Enjoy your meal, Mr. Blade."

When the door shut behind him, Justin took his seat. "I thought you hadn't had dinner."

"I'm not hungry," she said simply.

With a shrug Justin applied himself to the salad and tasted nothing. "Apparently there were no major problems while I was gone."

"Nothing I couldn't handle. Though I do have a few personal suggestions, I feel the hotel and the casino run very smoothly."

"You made a good investment." He sliced through the meat.

"You could look at it that way." Serena draped an arm over the back of the couch. Her beaded jacket shimmered in the quiet light. Looking at her, Justin wanted nothing more than to drag it off her, and the thin black silk she wore beneath, to lose himself in her again, the soft white skin, the masses of gold hair. He stabbed a piece of steak with his fork.

"The hotel seems to have gotten over the hump in this last year," he said easily. "It seems unnecessary for both of us to give it twenty-four hours a day." Unable to swallow any more, he poured coffee. "You might want to think about going back home."

She held the glass halfway to her lips. "Home?" she repeated dully.

"You're not needed here at the moment," he went on. "It occurred to me that it would be more practical for you to go home, or wherever you like, then come back and take over when I have to be away."

"I see." Blindly, she set the glass on the table in front of her and rose. "I've no intention of falling into the category of silent partner, Justin." Her voice was strong and clear, but from across the room he could see her eyes swim. "Nor do I have the intention of falling into the category of excess baggage. It's a very simple matter to go back to our original agreement and forget a one-night mistake." Because she could feel her hand begin to tremble, she reached for her drink again and drained it. "I'll pack my things and move back into my own suite."

"Damn it, Serena, I want you to go home." Watching her fight back tears, he felt something twist inside his stomach. In defense Justin pushed away from the table and strode down to her. "I don't want you here."

He heard her quick indrawn breath, but the mist in her eyes cleared with it. He found the dry-eyed, wounded look a hundred times worse. "There's no need to be cruel, Justin," she murmured. "You've made yourself clear. I'll get out of your rooms, but I own half this hotel, and I'm staying."

"I haven't signed the agreement yet," he reminded her.

She stared at him for a long silent moment. "You're that desperate to get rid of me," she murmured. "My mistake." Serena stared down at the empty glass in her hands. "If I'd been smarter, I wouldn't have slept with you until it was finalized."

Enraged, he grabbed the glass from her hand and hurled it across the room, where it shattered against the wall. "No!" Dragging her against him, he buried his face in her hair and swore again. "I can't do it this way. I won't let you think that."

Rigid with hurt, Serena didn't struggle. "Please let me go."

"Serena, listen to me. Listen to me," he repeated as he drew her away with his hands tight on her shoulders. "There was a letter delivered before I left Vegas. It was addressed to me, personally. Whoever planted that bomb wanted me to know he wasn't finished. He's going to hit me again—sometime, somewhere. There's more than money involved, I can feel it. It's personal, do you understand? You're not safe with me."

She stared at him as the words cut through the pain. "You said those things to me because you think I might be in some kind of danger if I stay?"

"I want you away from this."

Reaching up, Serena pushed his hands from her shoulders. "You're no better than my father," she said furiously. "Arranging my life with your little plots and schemes. Do you know what you did to me?" Tears threatened again and she forced them back. "Do you know how you hurt me? Did you ever consider just telling me the truth?"

"I've told you," he retorted, struggling against waves of guilt and need. "Now will you go?"

"No."

"Serena, for God's sake—"

"You expect me to pack my bags and run?" she interrupted, shoving at him in frustration. "To hide because someone *might* plant a bomb in the hotel *sometime?* Why don't you just ask me to find a nice little glass ball somewhere and take up residence? Damn it, Justin, I have as much at stake in this as you do."

"The hotel's fully covered by insurance. If anything happened, you wouldn't lose your investment."

She closed her eyes on a sigh. "You idiot."

"Serena, be reasonable."

When her eyes opened, the fury was back in them. "You're being reasonable, I suppose."

"I don't give a damn if I'm being reasonable or not!" he tossed back. "I want you somewhere where I know nothing can touch you."

"You can't *know* anything!"

"I know that I love you!" He grabbed her again, shaking her. "I know that you mean more to me than anything else in my life, and I'm not going to take any chances."

"Then how can you ask me to go away!" she shouted. "People in love belong together."

They stared at each other as each realized what had been said. Justin's grip gentled, then his hands dropped away. "Do this for me, Serena."

"Anything else," she answered. "Not this."

Turning, he paced to the window. Outside, the sun was sinking into the sea. Flashes of fire, streaks of gold—just like the woman behind him. "I've never loved anyone," Justin murmured. "My parents, my sister perhaps, but they've been out of my life a long time. I managed without them. I don't think I could manage without you. Even the thought that something might happen terrifies me."

"Justin." Going to him, Serena wrapped her arms around him and pressed her cheek to his back. "You know there're no guarantees, only odds."

"I've played the odds all my life. Not with you."

"I still make my own choices," she reminded him. "You can't change that, Justin. I can't let you. Tell me again," she demanded before he could answer. "And this time don't shout it at me. I'm as susceptible to romance as the next person."

When he turned back to her, Justin traced the curve of her lips with his fingertip. "I always thought *I love you* sounded so ordinary—until now." He replaced his fingertip with his lips, with the same gentle touch. "I love you, Serena."

She sighed as she felt him slip the jacket from her shoulders. "Justin," she murmured when he lifted her into his arms.

"Hmm?"

"Let's not tell my father. I hate it when he gloats."

Laughing, he lowered her to the bed.

He was going to love her gently. It seemed right somehow when he remembered the hurt in her eyes. She was precious to him, vital to his life, a permanent part of his thoughts. Soft and already warm, she drew him to her. He was going to love her gently, but she drove him mad.

Her hands were already pushing his robe aside, moving over his skin. Her lips were already racing over his face, nipping at his—teasing, tormenting, demanding. Justin swore as he pulled the dress down her body, and the sound of her low, husky laughter pushed him over the edge. Perhaps he hurt her; he couldn't control his hands. They were wild to touch, to possess. But she only arched beneath him, wanton, with abandon, until the blood roared like thunder in his ears. He murmured mindlessly in the tongue of his ancestors—threats, promises, phrases of love and war he could no longer separate.

Serena heard the harsh, quiet words—words both

primitive and erotic when whispered against her skin. There was nothing of the smooth sophisticated gambler in him now, but something fierce and untamed. And he was hers, she thought wildly as his hands bruised over her. She smelled his rich male scent, a scent undiluted by colognes, and buried her face against his shoulder, wanting to absorb it. But his hunger would allow her no leisure. Hot and open, his mouth crushed down on hers, demanding not surrender, but aggression.

Desire me, he seemed to say. *Need me.* She answered with a torrent of passion that left them both gasping. She thought he'd shown her everything there was to know, everything there was to have, in their first night of loving. How could there be so much more with still a promise of secrets as yet undiscovered? He seemed to have a depthless well of energy and need. As he had from the very beginning, he challenged her to match it.

He touched her, and a hundred small, violent explosions erupted inside her. As her body shuddered from them, all her girlhood imaginings of lovemaking—the tender words, the soft touches—paled into insignificance. This is what she'd been meant for: the tempest and the fury.

With mouths desperately clinging, they joined into one wild, insatiable form.

With her eyes still closed Serena stretched luxuriously. "Oh, God, I feel wonderful!" Even to her own ears her voice sounded like the purr of a contented cat.

"I've often thought so," Justin agreed, and ran a hand down the length of her.

With a laugh she sat up, stretching her arms high

over her head. In the half light he watched her hair tumble over her naked back as it arched. "No, I really do . . . if it weren't for the fact that I'm starving."

"You said you weren't hungry," he reminded her. Reaching up, he hooked an arm around her waist and brought her falling back onto the bed.

"I wasn't." She rolled on top of him. "Now I am." After nibbling kisses over his face, she nipped at his lip. "Famished."

"You can have the rest of my steak."

"It's cold," she complained. With a sultry laugh she pressed her mouth to his throat. "Can't you think of something else?"

"I admire your spirit," he said, bringing her lips back to his. After running a hand down her hair, he cradled her head on his shoulder. "Want me to call room service?"

She let out a long, contented breath. "In a little while. I love you, Justin."

As he closed his eyes, his arm tightened around her. "I wondered if you'd get around to telling me that."

"Didn't I mention it?" Smiling, Serena propped herself on his chest. "How's this? I love you," she began, punctuating her words with kisses. "I adore you. I'm fascinated by you. I lust for you."

"It might do for a start." Taking her hand to his lips, he kissed her fingers slowly. "Serena—"

"No." Quickly, she pressed her hand over his mouth. "Don't ask me again. I'm not going anywhere, and I don't want to fight with you, Justin. Not now, not tonight." She touched her cheek to his. "It seems like I've waited all of my life to feel like this. Everything up to this moment seems like a prelude. It sounds crazy, but I think I knew the first minute I looked up and saw you that everything was going to change." She laughed again and drew away. "And I thought I was much too intellectually sound to believe in love at first sight."

"Your intellect," he told her, "slowed things down considerably."

"On the contrary," she said with a haughty smile. "It moved them along beautifully. I came here with the idea of becoming your partner so that we could deal on equal terms while I convinced you you couldn't live without me."

"Did you?"

She grinned down at him. "It worked."

"You might be a bit too cocky, Serena." Giving her hair a tug, he rose from the bed.

"Where are you going?"

"To let a little air out of your balloon." Opening a drawer, Justin drew out a small box. "I picked this up for you in St. Thomas."

"A present?" Scrambling up on her knees, she held out her hand. "I live for presents."

"Greedy little witch," he said as he dropped the box into her outstretched hand.

Her chuckle faded into silence as she opened it. Twin pinwheels of amethysts and diamonds gleamed up at her, catching fire even in the dim light of dusk. She remembered how they had looked in the sunlit window where she had first seen them. Hesitantly, she touched one with her finger as if the heat were real and not just an illusion in the stones.

"Justin, they're gorgeous," she whispered as she raised her eyes to his. "But why?"

"Because they suited you, and you wouldn't indulge yourself. And"—he dropped a hand to her cheek—"I'd already decided I wasn't going to let you walk out of my life. If you hadn't come here, I'd have brought you."

"Willing or not?" she asked with the beginnings of a smile.

"I warned you it's an old tradition in my family." He tucked her hair behind her ears. "Put them on. I've wondered how they'd look on you."

Serena took them out of the box and clipped them to her ears. Still kneeling on the bed, she caught her hair back in her hand. "I want to see." Justin stopped her with no more than a look.

Her skin was pale and flawless. Her hair, when her hand slowly dropped, tumbled wildly. Wearing no more than the glitter of jewels at her ears, she looked like an exotic fantasy. The flare of desire in his eyes touched off one in her own. As her lips parted, she held out her arms to him.

Chapter Ten

Serena stretched luxuriously and contemplated getting up. If Justin hadn't already gone downstairs, the idea of lazing away the morning in bed would have been more appealing. She lay in the center of the tangle of sheets—the spot they had shared, wrapped close, throughout the night.

He was still worried, she mused. Even though he'd whispered nothing more than a few foolish endearments into her ear before he had left her, Serena had sensed the controlled tension in him. As long as Justin was convinced the bomb planted in Vegas had been a direct threat against him personally, and a prelude of more, there was nothing Serena could do to soothe him. She could only stay close, trying to convince him she was in no danger, that she could look after herself.

Men, Serena thought with a small smile. No matter

how liberal, they simply couldn't accept the fact that women could take care of themselves. The last thing she was going to do was sit in Massachusetts while the man she loved sat in New Jersey. It wasn't logical, Serena told herself as she pulled herself out of bed. She believed exactly what she had shouted at Justin the night before—people in love belonged together.

Justin wasn't likely to relax fully until the police caught whoever had planted the bomb, and that could take months—if indeed he were ever caught. He might have given up completely when his plans were ruined. Or he could wait—days, weeks, months—before striking again.

Taking a robe out of the closet, she considered that possibility, then shrugged off the unease. Whether they caught him or not, Serena didn't share Justin's certainty that the man would try again. The note had probably been sent out of frustration after the extortionist's plans had fallen apart. That made more sense than someone with a personal vendetta against Justin.

He just wasn't being objective, Serena decided as she belted the robe. The hotels were so much a part of him, he couldn't see them as an outsider would—buildings worth a great deal of money. The man had played his hand and lost. He had to know the authorities would be investigating, and that Justin would tighten his own security. Cowards plant bombs, she told herself. A coward isn't going to risk getting caught. In time, Justin would see the logic.

When she heard the knock on the door, Serena automatically checked the bedside clock. Too early for the maid, she reflected as she walked into the living room. Now, who would be . . . Her hand paused on the knob as all of Justin's words of the night before ran through her head. *Someone's after me. You're not safe.*

Suddenly uneasy, Serena peered through the peephole. There, you see, she told herself as her nerves drained away. It's just foolishness. Opening the door, she grinned at her brother.

"You must have lost quickly last night if you're up this early," she commented.

Caine stared at her a moment before he stepped into the room. "It's not that early," he countered, glancing around. "I came up to see Justin."

"You've just missed him." Serena closed the door and tossed back her sleep-tumbled hair. "He went down to his office about fifteen minutes ago. Where's Alan?"

Caine's affection for Justin was warring with the fact that Serena was his sister. His *baby* sister, damn it, he thought. And she was standing in Justin's private suite wearing nothing but the short silk robe he'd given her last Christmas. "He's just having breakfast," Caine told her as he prowled around the room.

"Well, you were always the one to be up and about in the morning," Serena remembered. "I always thought it was a disgusting habit. Want some coffee? It's one of the few essentials stocked in the kitchen."

"Yeah. Sure." Still dealing with the shock of realizing he had harbored the illusion that his sister was exclusively *his* sister, Caine followed her.

The kitchen was roomy and striking. The floor and walls were white, the cabinets glossy black. Serena plugged in the percolator as she gestured toward the breakfast bar with her free hand. "Sit down."

"You seem to know your way around," Caine heard himself saying.

She sent him an infuriatingly amused look. "I live here."

Annoyed, Caine slid onto a stool at the bar. "Justin certainly works fast."

"That's quite a chauvinistic remark for the liberal state's attorney," Serena commented as she measured out coffee. "From another point of view it could be said I work fast."

"You met him only a month ago."

"Caine." Turning around, Serena cocked her head. "Do you remember Luke Dennison?"

"Who?"

"He was the local stud when I was fifteen," she reminded him. "You cornered him in the parking lot of the movie theater and told him if he ever put his hands on me, you'd break all the small, vital bones in his body."

She watched Caine's grin flash as he remembered. "He never did, did he?"

"No." Then she walked over to him and grabbed both his ears. "I'm not fifteen anymore, Caine, and Justin isn't Luke Dennison."

Leaning over, he grabbed her ears in turn, applying enough pressure to bring her closer. "I love you," he told her, and kissed her quick and hard.

"Then be happy for me. Justin's everything I want."

Releasing her, Caine sat back. "He said the same thing about you."

He saw the pleasure darken her eyes. "When?"

"Yesterday, when he asked Alan and me to talk you into going home for a while." Caine lifted a hand as the pleasure turned to temper. "Don't go for the jugular, Rena; we both declined."

Serena let out her breath in a quick huff. "Justin's convinced whoever planted that bomb had more than extortion money as a motive. Because of that, he has it fixed in his head that I'm not safe with him." Frustrated, she gestured widely with both hands. "He just won't be logical or practical about the whole business."

"He loves you."

The storm around her stilled instantly. "I know. All the more reason for me to stay with him. Tell me," she leaned back against the counter to watch him, "what would you do?"

"If I were Justin, I'd do my damnedest to make you leave. If I were you," he continued smoothly before she could start to yell, "I wouldn't budge."

"Nothing worse than the analytical, legal mind," Serena murmured as the coffee perked. "Well, why don't you tell me what you've been doing with yourself? Any fascinating new ladies—or is your work cramping your style?"

"I manage to eke out a little time for recreation," he commented, and earned a snort as Serena took down two mugs. "I've decided to go back to private practice."

"You have?" Surprised, she turned back. "Isn't that rather sudden?"

"Not really." He accepted the mug of black coffee. "I've been thinking about it for some time. Alan's the politician. He's got the patience for it." Shrugging, Caine sipped at his coffee. "I miss the courtroom. Bureaucracy doesn't give me enough time for it."

"I always loved to watch you argue a case," Serena remembered, taking her seat on the opposite side of the bar. "There was something deadly about your style, like a wolf circling a fire and losing patience."

Caine laughed. "There's that flighty MacGregor imagination surfacing again."

"Casting aspersions on the family name?" Alan asked from the kitchen doorway.

Serena turned to him with a quick warm smile. The look altered subtly as she shifted her eyes to the man beside her brother.

"Alan complained that he'd been deserted," Justin commented. "Any more of that coffee?"

"I just made it." She held out her hand to him as he entered. Taking it, Justin brushed a kiss over her fingers before he moved to the coffeepot.

"Alan?"

He was looking at his sister. "Yes, thanks."

"Caine hasn't told me how much he lost last night," Serena began as Alan leaned on the counter.

"Oh, his luck wasn't all that bad." He sent his brother a shrewd look, which Caine returned blandly.

Serena arched a brow. "You better not have been trying your *luck* with any of my dealers," she warned Caine.

"The little blonde," Alan supplied with a flashing grin, "with the big brown eyes."

"Caine!" Serena sent him a look of astonished amusement. "She's barely twenty-one."

"I don't know what he's talking about." Calmly, Caine sipped his coffee. "Alan was busy trying to impress some redhead in half a dress with his views on foreign policy."

"Well." Serena turned to Justin as he brought over fresh coffee. "It seems to me that neither the staff nor the customers are safe if we let these two loose."

"You can keep an eye on them tonight at the dinner show." Justin handed Alan a mug before he opened the refrigerator for cream.

"I should have warned you," Serena told her brothers as she linked her hand with Justin's. "He has a habit of making arrangements without consulting anyone. But I for one," she added, smiling at him, "would love to go to the dinner show. Lena Maxwell's opening tonight," she mused, looking down at her nails. "I suppose Justin could be persuaded to introduce her if you two would like to come."

"What time's dinner?" Alan and Caine asked together.

Laughing, Serena rose. "Pitiful. Dangle a sexy brunette in front of their noses and they'll follow you anywhere. I've got to shower and change." She stood on her toes and brushed Justin's mouth with hers. "I'll be downstairs in a half hour."

As she walked from the room, she heard Caine's question. "Just where is Lena Maxwell rehearsing this afternoon, Justin?"

While she showered, Serena found herself laughing. If Caine got it into his head to track down Lena Maxwell, he wouldn't need Justin's introduction to charm his way into a personal conversation with her.

Caine MacGregor had more than his fair share of charm.

She thought again of his reaction when he found her in Justin's suite. It was rather endearing really, she decided. And she hadn't missed the long, quiet look Alan had given her when he had walked into the kitchen with Justin. As soon as her brothers were alone, she concluded, they would discuss her relationship with Justin, probably argue a bit about it, then give her their unqualified support. It had always been that way among the three of them.

For a moment, with the water streaming hot over her body, Serena felt a wave of regret for Justin. He had never really known the security, the bond, the frustration, of family ties. Perhaps with time he would let her show him. Perhaps one day they would have children.

Deliberately, Serena stuck her head under the spray. She was getting ahead of herself. Far ahead. He loved her, but that didn't mean he was looking for marriage and children. He'd been solitary for so long, and their love was so new. Children would mean a home, and he'd never chosen to make one. He'd chosen a lifestyle without permanence. And the nomad in him had been, and was, part of his attraction for her. It was foolish to start dreaming about changes when they'd barely lived forty-eight hours under the same roof.

Yet, he'd spoken of his sister twice, and both times Serena had sensed a hint of regret. Justin hadn't turned his back on his family, but had been forced by circumstances to do without. If one day he wanted one, Serena promised herself, she'd be there for him.

Stepping from the shower, Serena flicked on the

overhead heat lamp, then wrapped her hair in a towel. She began to hum as she rubbed scented lotion over her skin. Briefly, she ran over the scheduling she'd outlined for herself that day and decided she could accomplish everything before she needed to change for the dinner show. But not if she stood loitering in the bathroom all day, she reminded herself as she slipped into her robe. Unwinding the towel from her hair, she walked back into the bedroom.

As the door from the living room swung open, she gasped in surprise. "Justin!" Dragging a hand through her hair, Serena let out her breath. "You gave me a start; I thought you'd gone."

Dipping his hands into his pockets, he looked at her slowly, from her toes to the crown of her head. "No."

Why was it, she wondered, that he's seen and touched every part of my body but he can look at me like that and turn me to jelly? "Alan and Caine?"

"Gone down to compete for Lena, I believe."

"Lord, I hate to miss that," she thought aloud as she walked to the closet.

"What are you doing?"

"Well, I'm getting dressed," she returned with a laugh. "What does it look like I'm doing?"

"Seems like a waste of time, since I'm just going to take whatever you put on off you again."

She sent him an arched look over her shoulder. "Somehow, I think Kate might find it odd if I walked into the office wearing my robe."

He gave her a slow, cool smile. "You're not getting out of this room."

"Justin, don't be ridiculous." With another laugh

Serena began to poke through the clothes in the closet. "I have a dozen things to do before dinner, and—" The rest of the words caught in her throat, then came out as a whoosh of air as he tossed her onto the mattress.

Standing above her, he nodded. "I like the way you look in a rumpled bed."

"Oh, really?" Serena pushed herself up to her knees. "Well, I'd like to know where you got the idea you could throw me around." As she stuck her hands on her hips, her loosened robe fell off one shoulder. "It's not the first time," she went on, remembering her dunking in the ocean, "but if you think you can make a habit—"

"I know, nobody pushes a MacGregor around," he murmured as he hooked a finger in the opening of her robe.

"That's right." She pushed his hand away and succeeded in widening the gap down her front. "So just remember that the next time you get a wild urge to toss me around."

"I will. Sorry." With an apologetic smile he held out his hand. Though wary, Serena accepted it as she started to climb back out of the bed. In an instant she was on her back, pinned under him.

"Justin!" Fighting against laughter, she pushed at him. "Will you stop? I have to get dressed."

"Uh-uh, you have to get undressed. Let me help you." With one long gesture of his hand he parted her robe completely.

"*Stop!*" Amused, frustrated, and aroused, she struggled against him. "Justin, I mean it! The maid could walk in here any minute."

"She won't be coming until this evening." He found

a spot, low on her ribs, and felt a thrill of pleasure as she moaned. "I called housekeeping."

"You—" With a new spurt of energy she tried to wrest free. "You did it again!" She nearly managed to get her arms free before he pinned them. "Didn't it occur to you that I might have had plans? That perhaps I don't *want* to spend the afternoon in bed with you?"

"I figured the odds were good that I could persuade you," he countered easily.

"Oh!" She kicked out, tangling her legs with his as she wiggled under him.

"Okay, we'll wrestle first, best three out of five."

"This isn't funny," she said, swallowing a giggle. "I mean it."

"Deadly serious." He rolled her over until she was on top of him. "That's one apiece." Before she could catch her breath she was back under him. "And two for me."

"Oh, sure." Serena blew the wet hair out of her eyes. "A real even match when I'm half naked and you're fully dressed."

"You're right." He covered her face with quick, teasing kisses. "Why don't you do something about that. My hands are busy."

She moaned involuntarily as they ran down her body. "Foul," she said breathlessly. "Justin . . ."

"Stop?" he asked halfheartedly, his eyes intent on her face as he let his fingertips do the persuading.

"No." Tangling her fingers in his hair, she brought his mouth down to hers.

It was always the same, always unique. Every time his lips met hers, she felt that enervating shock of heat.

Her bones would soften with exquisite slowness until she thought her body was one warm, fluid mass. Yet the thrill was always fresh, as though it were happening for the first time. Forgetting his request that she undress him, Serena went lax with the first flood of pleasure.

Justin felt her surrender, a surrender he knew was only a prelude to her breathless excitement and frantic demands. He enjoyed the brief, heady power of total control. She was his now, a strong, vital woman who for a few precious moments would be like putty in his hands. The knowledge made him gentle, so that he caressed with more tenderness than he had believed himself capable of. Did love make so much difference? he wondered as he ran long, lean fingers over her skin.

His lips touched hers, muffling her soft sound of enjoyment. Her eyes, not quite closed, met his. When he traced the shape of her mouth with his tongue, her lids fluttered. He rubbed his lips over hers, savoring the taste, then he found that his hands had stilled. His whole being seemed focused on the meeting of mouth to mouth. The power he had felt became a vulnerability, no less of a surrender than Serena had given him. He felt weak with it, and fearless.

"I love you," he murmured against her mouth. "I didn't know how much." The kiss was deep and slow and more arousing than anything he'd ever known.

Then her tongue sought his, moving through his lips to draw in all the tastes and flavors. As a shudder passed through him, he knew her surrender was over.

Serena slipped the soft wool of his sweater up his torso, over his shoulders, so that their lips were forced to part, but only briefly. Her hands were busy, touching, rubbing, demanding. He could see them in his mind's eye, smooth and white against his darker skin, the glossy feminine nails scraping over him in excitement. He moved his lips to her shoulder to nip gently, and was assaulted by her scent. It made him think of sultry summer nights, wild loving in high green grass. He ran kisses, grown more desperate, to the inside of her elbow, where her rapid pulse only intensified the fragrance. As he buried his mouth against the pale, blue-veined skin, her body arched, tossed by passion.

Serena rolled to him so that they were side by side, then locked her arms around him. She didn't feel the tangle of sheets beneath her, the cool silk of her robe that had slipped down to her legs. All she felt was his hard, hot body aginst hers and the moist, tingling path his mouth streaked over her.

As he slid down she urged him toward all the secret places he'd discovered for both of them. No one else would ever bring her this torrid, wanton hunger. It filled her, consumed her, made her strong. With a sudden burst of energy she was on top of him, her mouth greedy, her hands quick and clever. He groaned, gripping her wet, sleek hair. The sound only made her move over him more urgently. He's beautiful, so beautiful, was all she could think as she touched and tasted and touched again.

A light film of sweat glistened on his dark skin. Serena could taste the saltiness of it as she roamed over the hard, smooth chest, the lean line of ribs marred by the jagged scar, the narrow, long-boned hips.

Then his hands gripped her, dragging her up until his mouth was fastened on hers. She drew in the mingling flavor of their tastes until her head swam with it. Her body seemed to act without her knowledge, sliding down until she took him inside of her. The sensation rocketed through her, causing her to cry out as she arched back. But he rose up with her, his hands still gripping her hair, his mouth still fused to hers. She couldn't breathe, but even as she fought for air, her body set up its own raging rhythm.

Her arms were locked around him, his around her. The mutual grip tightened convulsively as they reached the sharp, airless summit, then as one form they slid back to the bed to lay gasping.

"I can't seem to get enough of you," Justin managed in a whisper. "Never enough."

"Don't." Serena let her head slip limply to her shoulder. "Don't ever get enough."

They lay quietly as breathing settled and trembles eased. With her palm over his heart, she could feel the pounding beat become slow, strong, and steady.

"There's only you," Justin said, feeling the sudden fierceness of love. "There's only you in my life."

Serena lifted her head to look down at him. "'Love that is not madness is not love.'" Smiling, she traced the line of his cheekbone. "I never understood that until now. I know I never want to be sane again."

He brought her finger to his lips. "So the brainy Serena MacGregor chooses insanity."

Wrinkling her nose, she folded her elbows over his chest. "No need to bring my brain into it."

"It fascinates me," Justin told her. "And it's one part of you I haven't really explored. Just how smart are you?"

She lifted a brow. "That," she said primly, "is an abstract question."

"Ah, you're going to be evasive." Grinning, he brushed her hair away from her shoulders. "How many degrees do you have?"

"Your first question doesn't have anything to do with your second. How smart are you?"

"Smart enough to know when I'm getting the runaround," he said mildly. "No burning desire to go into law or politics like your brothers?"

"No. My only burning desire was to learn. Then I had a burning desire to be doing. Now"—she bit his lower lip—"I have more basic burning desires."

"Hmmm." He allowed himself the pleasure of feasting on her mouth a moment. "Don't you feel that running a gambling hotel is a bit of a waste of your education?"

"Of course not. My education's mine, I'll always have it whatever I choose to do. What good are degrees if you're not enjoying your life?" With a sigh she lay across his chest again. "I didn't study so that I could pile up little pieces of paper suitable for framing, but because I was curious. Why do you run hotels?"

"Because I'm good at it."

Serena grinned at him. "And that's the exact reason I nearly became a professional student. But it was becoming too repetitious and too easy. There're challenges here every day and a constant variety of people. And," she added smugly, "I'm good at it too."

"Nero thinks you have class."

Now Serena's smile was just as smug as her voice.

"He's very perceptive. Why didn't you make him manager?"

"He wasn't interested." Justin began to run a hand up and down her spine. "He likes his position as unofficial troubleshooter. I'll be sending him to Malta next year."

"You've bought the casino then?"

"I will have soon enough." Thoughtfully, he studied her face. "I was considering taking on a partner."

He saw the smile light in her eyes just before her lips curved. "Were you? Then I suppose I should put in my bid right away."

He cupped his hand around the back of her neck. "The sooner the better," he murmured as he brought her lips to his.

When the phone rang, he swore ripely. Serena laughed and nuzzled against his throat as he reached for it.

"Blade." Listening to Kate's quiet, shaking voice, he fought to keep the tension out of his body. Serena would feel it. "All right, Kate, I'll be down." After hanging up he kissed the crown of Serena's head. "Something's come up downstairs."

She gave a resigned sigh. "That's the trouble with living where you work." Rolling over, she stretched. "Well, I really should go down myself."

"You haven't had a day off in over a week." Dressing, Justin wondered if he was wiser to leave her there or to keep her with him downstairs. He decided she'd be better off in the penthouse. "Relax for a while, I'll be back up soon. Why don't you order some lunch?"

The thought of having him to herself all afternoon was too appealing. Serena closed her mind to the paperwork on her desk. "All right—an hour?"

"Yes, fine." Preoccupied, he headed for the elevator.

Kate was waiting for him when he stepped off. Silently, she handed Justin a plain white envelope.

"Steve found it lying on the front desk. As soon as I saw it . . ." She trailed off, then got control of herself. "It's just like the one you got in Vegas, isn't it?"

"Yes," Justin answered flatly as he studied the carefully executed block letters that spelled out his name. He had a quick, savage urge to simply rip it into pieces, but took a letter opener from his desk and carefully slit one edge. Sliding the note out, he unfolded it.

IT'S NOT OVER YET. YOU HAVE A PRICE TO PAY.

"Call security," he told Kate as he read the words a second time. Then he let out his breath on one violent oath. "And the police."

Chapter Eleven

Serena pulled a black angora sweater over her head. It would feel good to be lazy for a day, she decided, to lounge around the suite in comfortable clothes and do absolutely nothing. She and Justin hadn't spent a full day together since St. Thomas.

That made her think of the earrings Justin had given her. She'd wear them tonight, Serena mused as she opened the top drawer of the dresser to draw out the box. They're exquisite, she thought as she looked at them again. All the more exquisite because he had bought them for her then, before they had been lovers.

What a strange man he is, she reflected. So cool in some ways, so introspective, yet he was capable of such incredibly sweet gestures. The violets in her room the first day—champagne for breakfast. And underneath it all there was that latent, controlled streak of violence. All those aspects of him excited her.

How smart are you? Serena laughed as she remembered Justin's question. Smart enough to know I'm a very lucky woman, she answered silently. Reaching into the drawer again, she drew out a two-headed quarter she'd picked up while Justin had been in Vegas. With a grin Serena examined it, then slipped it into the pocket of her jeans. And smart enough to keep an ace up my sleeve, she added with a gleam of mischief in her eye.

As she glanced at her reflection in the mirror, Serena's grin turned to a look of astonishment. Her hair had dried in a tangled and unruly mop around her face. What a mess, she thought as she picked up her brush. Well, she'd do something about it before she called room service. It would serve Justin right if he had to wait for his lunch, she added as she tugged painfully at the knots in her hair. Bending from the waist, she let her hair fall forward, then gritted her teeth and brushed the underside.

"Ouch! Just a minute," she called out at the quick, quiet knock on the door. Either Caine or Alan had struck out with Lena Maxwell, she thought with a smirk as she headed for the door, still brushing her hair. "Don't expect me to fix you up with—oh."

"Housekeeping." A slim boy of about twenty gave her a shy smile.

Justin must have decided to have them clean before

lunch, she concluded. Typical. He might have called to let her know.

"I can come back later if—"

"Oh, no, I'm sorry. I was thinking of something else." Serena gave him a smile as she opened the door wide enough for him to roll the maid's cart inside. "You're new, aren't you?"

"Yes, ma'am, this is my first day."

That explains the nervous swallowing, she decided, and made her smile warmer. "Just relax and take your time," she advised him. "I'll stay out of your way." Gesturing with her brush, she turned away. "Why don't you start in the kitchen while I—"

Something clamped over her mouth and nose. Too stunned to be frightened, Serena grabbed at the hand as she drew her breath to shout. She inhaled something strong and cloyingly sweet that made her head spin. Recognizing the scent, she began to struggle more frantically, fighting the mists that were whirling in front of her eyes.

Oh, God, no. Her arms dropped heavily to her sides, the brush slipped from her limp fingers. Justin . . .

"The desk clerk found it on the counter," Justin told Lieutenant Renicki. "Apparently, no one saw who put it there. It was during checkout time, and the desk staff was busy."

"Yes. Well, he's not a fool." The police lieutenant picked up the plain sheet of stationery by the corner and slipped it into a plastic bag. "I'll have to turn this over to the Bureau, I imagine, but for now I'll leave a few plainclothesmen in the hotel."

"I've my own security stationed in all the public rooms."

Lieutenant Renicki lifted both of his bushy, graying brows in acknowledgment. Doesn't like dealing with me, he decided. Oh, he's a cool one. He watched Justin light a cigar with rock-steady hands. Not much gets under that one's skin.

"Got any enemies, Mr. Blade?"

Justin shot him a mild look. "Apparently."

"Anyone specific you want to tell me about?"

"No."

"Is this the first threat you've received since you got back from Nevada?"

"Yes."

Lieutenant Renicki suppressed a sigh. Characters like Blade made him feel like a dentist yanking at a reluctant tooth. "Hired or fired anyone recently?"

For an answer, Justin pushed his intercom. "Kate, check with personnel. See who we've put on or let go in the last two months. Then get a printout from the rest of the hotels."

"Great things, computers," the lieutenant said when Justin hung up. "I got a teenager practically married to one." Getting no response, he shrugged his rounded shoulders. "I'm going to check your security myself. If he's going to plant a bomb, he has to get in first."

"He can get in," Justin reminded him, "by signing a name at the registration desk."

"True enough." Lieutenant Renicki watched the cigar smoke drift. "You can close down."

The only change in Justin's expression was a fractional narrowing of his eyes. "No."

"Didn't think so." Lieutenant Renicki hauled himself out of the chair. "My men will be discreet, Mr. Blade, but we'll make a routine search. I'll check back with you after I've interviewed the desk clerks."

"Thank you, Lieutenant." Justin waited until the door closed behind him, then crushed out his cigar with a force that snapped it in two. If he'd felt a stalking sensation before, now he felt breathing down his neck. He was here now—if not in the hotel, then somewhere close. Waiting. Serena was going back to Hyannis Port if Justin had to tie her up and dump her on a plane.

He sat very still for a moment until he was calm again. He wouldn't get through to Serena by shouting or threatening. The only way would be to make her see that her presence there made it impossible for him to be completely rational. If she were gone, he could think clearly enough and perhaps reason out who and why. Justin lifted the intercom again.

"Kate, I'll be upstairs. Pass my calls through to me up there." Rising, he went to the elevator. Maybe on the way up he would think of the best way to tell Serena he was kicking her—and her brothers—out of his hotel.

As he stepped into the living room, Justin glanced toward the picture window, half expecting to see her sitting there, already nibbling at lunch. He was only vaguely surprised to see the table empty—he'd taken a bit more than the hour he'd allotted. Thinking perhaps she'd fallen back to sleep, Justin walked into the bedroom. The rumpled bed didn't bring on a twinge of desire this time but a feeling of unease. Calling her name, Justin walked toward the bathroom.

The faintest wisp of her scent clung to the air. Because the room was empty, it only made Justin's unease sharpen. Don't be an idiot, he told himself. She isn't tied to this suite. She could have gone out for a hundred reasons. But she was expecting me. She would have phoned down. How did he know? As he walked back out into the living room, Justin reminded himself that they hadn't been together long enough to be sure of the other's habits. She could have run down to the boutique for a dress.

Bending, Justin picked up the small, enamel-handled brush from the rug. For a moment his mind went blank, and he could do no more than stare at it. He shook himself clear. He was being an alarmist—she'd come walking back in any moment. It was like her to leave her things all over the suite. To be untidy, he mused mercilessly. Not careless. Picking up the phone, Justin punched a number.

"Page Serena MacGregor."

He held the brush as he waited. Her beaded jacket hung over the back of the sofa. He could remember slipping it from her shoulders the night before. Sometime during the morning she had picked it up and tossed it there. Then why would she have left her brush on the floor?

"Ms. MacGregor doesn't answer the page, sir."

Justin felt the knot in his stomach tighten. He gripped the handle of the brush until it threatened to snap. "Page Alan or Caine MacGregor." Glancing at his watch, Justin saw that it was thirty minutes past the time he had told Serena to expect him.

"Caine MacGregor."

"It's Justin. Is Serena with you?"

"No, Alan and I were—"

"Have you seen her?"

"Not since this morning." It was the first time in the ten years he had known Justin, Caine realized, that he'd heard a hint of panic in that controlled voice. Something like ice rippled down his back. "Why?"

Justin found his throat closed and stared down at the brush in his hand. "She's gone."

Caine felt the receiver grow wet under his palm. "Where are you?"

"Upstairs."

"We'll be right there."

Within minutes Justin opened the door to admit Serena's brothers. "She might've gone out for something," Caine said immediately. "Did you check to see if she took her car out?"

"No." Justin cursed himself and picked up the phone again. "This is Blade. Has Ms. MacGregor taken her car out?" He waited, angry, impatient, while Caine prowled the room and Alan watched him. Justin listened to the answer from the garage, then hung up without speaking. "Her car's still there."

"She might have gone for a walk on the beach," Alan suggested.

"She was expecting me here a half hour ago," Justin said flatly. "She was supposed to order some lunch, but I've checked; she never called down. I found this near the front door."

Alan took the brush from Justin's hand. He remembered giving the antique vanity set to Serena for her sixteenth birthday. It was one of the few things she owned that she took meticulous care of.

"Had you been arguing?"

Justin whirled on Caine as his control slipped another notch.

"Justin," Caine said quickly. "Rena has a wicked temper. If she were angry, she could have stormed out without a word to anyone. She'd stomp around on the beach until she'd cooled off."

"No, we hadn't been arguing," Justin said tightly. "We'd been making love." He stuck his hands in his pockets because he wanted to ball them into fists. "I got a call from downstairs. An envelope had been left for me at the front desk. It was another threat."

Alan set Serena's brush down carefully on the table. "Justin." He waited until the angry green eyes met his. "Call the police."

Like an exclamation point at the end of his words, the phone rang. Justin grabbed for it. "Serena," he began.

"Looking for her already?" The voice was muffled and sexless. "I've got your squaw, Blade." The connection broke with a soft click.

Justin stood still as a stone for a full ten seconds. He

tasted copper in his mouth and recognized it as fear. "He's got her," he heard someone say, then realized the voice was his own. On a blind wave of fury he ripped the phone out of the wall and threw it across the room. "The son of a bitch has her."

Lieutenant Renicki glanced around the living room of Justin's suite and decided it was warmer than he would have expected. The man he had met downstairs seemed suited to cold colors and straight lines. His eyes rested on the phone that lay drunkenly against the east wall. Well, still waters run deep, he supposed.

The tall blond man staring out of the window was Caine MacGregor, the hotshot young lawyer who was currently serving as state's attorney in Massachusetts. The dark man sitting in the chair staring at the hairbrush in his hands was Alan MacGregor, U.S. senator, a bit of a left winger with a glib tongue. The lieutenant looked at Justin again.

"Suppose you run through it once more."

Justin's eyes leveled on Lieutenant Renicki's, full of fury and icy control. "I went downstairs to check out the envelope that had been left for me at the front desk. I left Serena here; it was just past noon. We made arrangements to have lunch here in the suite an hour later. I was late, and when I came back, she wasn't here. I was concerned, then when I found her hairbrush lying on the floor by the front door I had her paged. When she didn't answer, I paged her brothers. Fifteen minutes ago I received a call."

"Yes, apparently from a kidnapper," Renicki put in,

not certain if he was pleased or annoyed with Justin's cool recital. "You haven't told me precisely what he said."

Justin gave the lieutenant a long, intense look. "He told me he had my squaw."

Ready to explode, Caine whirled away from the window. "Damn it, this isn't getting us anywhere! Why aren't you looking for her?"

Lieutenant Renicki watched him with tired, patient eyes. "We're doing just that, Mr. MacGregor."

"He'll call again," Alan said quietly. He looked up from the hairbrush to meet the lieutenant's gaze. "He must know that between Justin and our family we can raise any amount of money to get Rena back." He let his eyes drift to Justin's and hold. "If his motive is money."

"We'll have to work on that premise for now, Senator," Lieutenant Renicki stated in a no-nonsense voice. "We'll be putting a tap on your phone, with your permission, Mr. Blade."

"Do whatever it takes."

Caine looked at Justin then, looked at him for the first time since the phone call. "Where's the brandy?"

"What?"

"You need a drink." When Justin merely shook his head, Caine let out a quiet oath. "Well, I'm going to have one—before I call Mom and Dad."

Justin felt a fresh twist inside his stomach and gestured. "In that cabinet."

From opposite ends of the suite the phone rang. Without waiting for Lieutenant Renicki's yes or no,

Justin went into the kitchen to answer. He couldn't bring himself to go into the bedroom. "Blade." Closing his eyes, he fought frustration, then held out the receiver. "It's for you," he told the lieutenant.

When he came back into the living room Justin found Alan and Caine standing in the center of the room, speaking quietly. "Alan's going to call our parents," Caine told him. "They'll take it better from him. They'll want to be here."

Justin struggled not to let the panic through, or the grief. "Of course."

As Lieutenant Renicki came into the room, he waited until all three pairs of eyes were on him. "My men found an abandoned maid's cart down in the garage. The lab will go over it thoroughly, but they found a rag soaked with ether inside. Apparently, that's how he got her out without anyone seeing her." Watching closely, Lieutenant Renicki saw Caine's knuckles whiten on his glass, saw the wave of terrified anger in Alan's eyes. He saw no change in Justin's expression. "We have your description of Miss MacGregor, Mr. Blade, but a picture would be helpful."

Justin stared as pain sprinted from his stomach to his throat. "I don't have one."

"I do." Numb, Alan reached for his wallet.

"We'll have the trace on the line right away, Mr. Blade," Lieutenant Renicki went on, glancing at the picture Alan had handed him. "We'll be recording everything that's said. The longer you keep him on the line, the better. Whatever demands he makes, insist on speaking to Miss MacGregor before you agree to anything. We have to establish that she is indeed with him." And alive, he added silently.

"And if he refuses?" Justin demanded.

"Then you refuse to deal."

Justin forced himself to sit down. If he stood, he would pace—if he paced, he would lose control. "No," he said evenly.

"Justin," Alan interrupted before Renicki could speak again. "The lieutenant's right. We have to be certain Rena is with him and unharmed." *It's Rena,* he thought wildly as he struggled to keep his voice even. *Our Rena.* "If you make it clear there won't be a ransom unless you hear her voice, he'll put her on the phone."

You have a price to pay. The words flashed through Justin's mind. Not Serena, he thought desperately. God, not Serena. "And after I've spoken to her," Justin began, "I'll agree to any terms he asks. I won't bargain, and I won't stall."

"It's your money, Mr. Blade." Lieutenant Renicki gave him a thin smile. "I'd like you to listen to his voice very carefully when he phones back. Chances are he has it disguised, but you might recognize a phrasing, an inflection."

There was a brisk knock on the door which the lieutenant answered himself. As he stood talking in undertones to one of his men, Caine again approached Justin with the offer of brandy. For the second time Justin shook his head.

"They're going to catch him," Caine said, just needing to hear the words aloud.

Slowly, Justin lifted his eyes. "When they do," he said calmly. "I'm going to kill him."

Feeling groggy and sore, Serena woke, moaning. Had she overslept? she wondered. She'd miss class if she didn't—no, no, it was her shift in the casino and Dale . . . Justin—no, Justin was coming up for lunch and she hadn't even called room service.

She had to get up, but her eyes refused to open and there was a light, rolling sense of nausea in her stomach. Sick, she thought hazily. But she was never sick. How . . . the door, she remembered. Someone at the door. Nausea welled again, and with it, fear. Drawing all her strength together, Serena opened her eyes.

The room was small and dim. Over the one window a shade was drawn. There was a cheap maple bureau against one wall with a mirror streaked with dust and a small, straight-back rocking chair. There was no lamp, only a ceiling fixture overhead. Because it was off and some light filtered through the shade, Serena knew it was still day. But her sense of time was so distorted, she had no idea which day.

Someone had once painted the walls an airy yellow, but the color had faded so that they now seemed more like the pages of a very old book. Serena lay in the middle of a double bed on top of a worn chenille spread. When she tried to move her right arm, she discovered that it was handcuffed to the center bedpost. That's when the fear overcame the grogginess.

The boy from housekeeping, she remembered. *Ether.* Oh, God, how could she have been so stupid!

Justin had warned her. . . . Justin, she thought again as she clamped down on her bottom lip. He'd be frantic by now. Was he searching for her? Had he called the police? Perhaps he thought she'd just gone out on an errand.

I have to get out of here, Serena told herself desperately and scrambled closer to the headboard to tug on the handcuffs. The boy must have had something to do with the bombing in Vegas. It seemed incredible. He looked barely old enough to shave. Old enough to kidnap, she reminded herself grimly, yanking uselessly at the metal cuffs. When she heard his footsteps, she sat very still and waited.

He'd planned it perfectly, Terry thought as he hung up the phone. Snatching the woman from under Blade's nose had been risky, but, oh, so worthwhile. Better than the bomb, he decided as he drummed his fingers against the table. He'd had to give them too much time and they'd found the bomb because he hadn't wanted to hurt anyone. Just Blade. But this— this was perfect.

She was beautiful, he mused. Blade would pay to get her back. But before he paid, he'd suffer. Terry was going to make sure of it. To relieve his own tension he reminded himself how clever he had been. Even while Justin had been in Vegas, Terry had been on his way to Atlantic City. At the time he'd been annoyed with himself for not choosing the East Coast hotel in the first place. But it had all worked out.

He'd noticed Serena the first night he'd hung around the casino—then he'd learned she was Justin's partner. It had only taken a few casual questions in the right places to learn she was much more than that to him. Then Terry had outlined his plan.

At first he'd been frightened. Getting a woman out of a hotel was trickier than getting a small bomb in. But he'd watched. No one looked twice at the people in the plain white housekeeping uniforms. After a couple of days of watching Serena's movements, he concluded there was a private entrance from the offices to the living quarters. Probably an elevator, he had reasoned. That was the way the rich did things. He'd been patient, spending most of his time at the slot machines, waiting.

When he'd seen Justin come back, he knew it was time to move. Stealing the uniform had been easy, as easy as planting the letter. No one took any notice of a young, harmless-looking man in plain clothes. The minute he had seen the desk clerk deliver the envelope to the offices, Terry had begun to move. He'd had to force himself to go slowly. He'd told himself to give Justin a full ten minutes to get downstairs. On the third floor he'd changed his clothes in a storage closet, then he'd simply walked off with one of the maid's carts that sat in the hallway.

He remembered how his heart had been pounding as he had wheeled into the service elevator. There was a chance that she wouldn't be there, that she'd gone down with Justin and he'd have to start all over again. When she had opened the door and smiled, he'd almost lost his nerve. Then he'd remembered Blade. The rest was easy.

It had taken him less than five minutes to cover her unconscious body with linen and wheel the cart down to the garage where his car was waiting. With Serena in the backseat, covered with a blanket, he'd simply driven away. But she'd been unconscious for a long time. Maybe he'd used too much ether, or . . . Then he heard her moan. Terry got up to fix her a cup of tea.

When he opened the door, Serena was sitting back against the headboard, staring at him. But she didn't look as frightened as he'd imagined she would. He wondered if she was in shock. He expected she'd start screaming any minute.

"If you yell," he said quietly, "I'll have to gag you. I don't want to do that."

Serena saw that he was holding a cup, and that it shook in his hand. A nervous kidnapper, she thought quickly, would be more dangerous than a calm one. She swallowed any urge to scream. "I won't yell."

"I brought you some tea." He came a little closer. "You might be feeling a little sick."

He was approaching her, Serena thought, as one approached a cornered animal. He expects me to be terrified, she realized. Well, he wasn't far off. It might be more to her advantage to let her control slip outwardly. Inside she'd force herself to be calm. The first thing she had to know was where he kept the keys for the handcuffs.

"I do. Please"—she let her voice tremble— "can I use the bathroom?"

"Okay, I'm not going to hurt you." He spoke soothingly as he set the tea aside and came to her. Taking a key from the pocket of his jeans, he fit it into the wrist lock. "If you try to run away or start yelling,

I'll have to stop you." He paused as his hand replaced the metal on her wrist. "Do you understand?"

Serena nodded. He was stronger, she discovered, than he looked.

Silently, he led her into a small bathroom. "I'm going to be right outside the door," he warned. "Just be smart and nothing'll happen to you."

Nodding, Serena went inside. Immediately, she looked for means of escape and was frustrated. There wasn't even a window. A weapon. A rapid search turned up nothing more than a towel bar that wouldn't budge. She bit down on her lip as fear and helplessness began to take over. She'd have to find another way. She *would* find another way.

Running cold water in the sink, she splashed it on her face. She had to stay calm and alert. And she couldn't underestimate the man outside the door. He was dangerous because he was every bit as frightened as she was. So she'd be more frightened, she decided. She would cower and weep so that he wouldn't know she was watching, waiting for the first opportunity of escape. First, she had to find out exactly what his plans were.

Opening the door, Serena let him seize her wrists again. "Please, what are you going to do?"

"I'm not going to hurt you," Terry said again as he pulled her toward the bed. "He'll pay to get you back."

"Who?"

She saw the fury in his eyes as he snapped the cuff back on her wrist. "Blade."

"My father has more," she began quickly. "He—"

"I don't want your father's money!" At his fierce explosion, Serena didn't have to simulate a shudder. "It's Blade. He's going to pay. I'm going to bleed him dry."

"Were you—were you the one who planted the bomb in Vegas?"

Terry handed her the tea. Serena considered throwing it into his face, then decided against it. If it were hot enough to burn him, he'd probably leap back and the key would be out of her reach.

"Yeah."

She watched him. There was angry color in his face now and a look in his eyes that had her stomach rolling. "Why?"

"He killed my father," Terry told her, then strode out of the room.

Why doesn't he call! Justin thought as he drank yet another cup of coffee. If he's hurt her— He looked down to see that he'd snapped the handle cleanly away from the mug. Setting them both down, he drew out a cigar. Behind him, in the dinette, two detectives played gin. Caine paced while Alan was already on his way to the airport to pick up Daniel and Anna. The living room extension had been repaired and was now attached to a recording device. But still they waited.

It was growing darker as clouds moved in. There'd be rain before the night was over. For God's sake, where was she! Why did I leave her alone? Justin wanted to bury his face in his hands. He wanted to hit something, anything. He sat perfectly still and stared at the wall. Why did I think she'd be safe here? he demanded of himself. I would have made her go away if I hadn't wanted her with me so badly. I could have made her go away. If anything happens to her . . .

He pushed the thought aside. If he were going to stay in control, he couldn't even allow himself the luxury of guilt. The only sounds in the room were the desultory conversation of the detectives and the hiss of Caine's lighter as he lit another cigarette. If the phone didn't ring, Justin was certain he'd go mad.

When it did, Justin lunged for it. "Keep him on the line as long as you can," one of the detectives ordered curtly. "And tell him you have to talk to her before you deal."

Justin didn't even acknowledge the instructions as he picked up the receiver. The recorder was running silently. "Blade."

"Want your squaw back, Blade?"

It was a young voice, Justin realized. And frightened. The same voice he had heard on the police recordings in Las Vegas. "How much?"

"Two million, cash. Small bills. I'll let you know when and where."

"Serena. Let me talk to Serena."

"Forget it."

"How do I know you have her?" Justin demanded. "How do I know she's . . ." He had to force the words out. "Still alive."

"I'll think about it."

And the line went dead.

Serena huddled under the blanket. She was cold. Scared, she corrected herself brutally. The chill she was feeling had nothing to do with her thin sweater or bare

feet. *He killed my father.* The flat statement ran over
and over in her head. Could this be the son of the man
who had attacked Justin all those years ago? He'd have
been little more than a baby at the time. If he'd been
harboring hate all those years . . . Serena shivered
again and drew the blanket over her shoulders.

She shouldn't have doubted Justin's instincts. He'd
known somehow that someone was after him personally. How far would the boy go for revenge? she asked
herself. Be objective, she ordered. This is real.

She'd seen his face. Could he take the chance of
letting her go when she could identify her? Yet, he
didn't seem like a cold-blooded killer. He'd planted a
bomb in a crowded hotel, she reminded herself. Oh,
God, she had to get away!

Closing her eyes, Serena put all her concentration
into listening. It was quiet, no sounds of traffic. She
thought, but couldn't be sure, that she heard the ocean.
It might've been the wind. How far out of town were
they? she wondered. If she threw the teacup through
the window and screamed, would anyone hear? Even
as she weighed the odds, Terry came back into the
bedroom.

"I brought you a sandwich."

He seemed more agitated this time, or perhaps, she
reconsidered, excited. Make him talk, she told herself.
"Please don't leave me alone." She grabbed his arm
with her free hand and let her eyes plead with his.

"You'll feel better after you eat," he mumbled, and
shoved the sandwich under her nose. "You don't have
to be scared. I told you I wouldn't hurt you if you didn't
try anything."

"I've seen you," she said, taking the chance. "How can you let me go?"

"I've got plans." Restless, he began to pace the little room. He wasn't big, she thought. If I could just get my hand free, I'd have a chance. "By the time I let them know where you are, I'll already be gone." He thought of Switzerland with grim pleasure. "They won't find me. I'll have two million dollars to help me hide in comfort."

"Two million," she whispered. "How do you know Justin will pay?"

Terry laughed, turning to look at her. Her face was pale, her eyes huge. Her hair tumbled wildly around her shoulders. "He'll pay. He'll beg me to let him pay before I'm finished."

"You said he killed your father."

"Murdered him."

"But he was acquitted. Justin told me—" The words slid back down her throat as Terry whirled.

"He murdered my father and they let him go!" he shouted. "Let him go because they felt sorry for him. It was all politics, my mother told me. They let him go because he was a poor Indian kid. My mother said that his lawyer paid off the witnesses."

His mother, Serena thought, had been warping his mind for years. It would take more than a few words from her to change it now. Had his mother told him about the scar along Justin's side? Had she told him his father had been drunk, or that the knife that had killed him had been his own? Serena studied Terry's set, frightened face and hating eyes. "I'm sorry," she said weakly. "I'm so sorry."

"He's paying now," Terry told her, and tossed a hank of errant hair out of his eyes. "I wish I could take the chance of holding you for more than a couple of days." He gave a soft, wondering laugh. "Who'd have thought I'd make Blade crawl for a woman?"

"Please, what's your name?"

"Terry," he said briefly.

Serena struggled to sit up straighter. "Terry, you must know Justin's called the police. They'll be looking for me."

"They won't find you," he returned simply. "I didn't start planning yesterday. I put a deposit down on this place six months ago, when Blade opened the hotel. I was thinking about squeezing him a second time after he'd paid off from Vegas." He shrugged as if the business in Vegas meant little. "The old couple I rented this from are in Florida by now. They've never even seen me, just the check I sent them."

"Terry—"

"Look, nothing's going to happen to you. Just eat and get some rest. Ten hours after Blade makes the drop, I'll call and let them know where to find you." He stormed out of the room, slamming the door before she could say any more.

"What are they doing to get her back!" Daniel demanded as he strode around the living room of Justin's suite. "Look at these two"—he tossed out a hand toward the two detectives—"playing cards while some maniac has my little girl."

"They're doing everything they can," Alan told him quietly. "The phone's tapped. He didn't stay on the line long enough last time to trace it. They're checking out all the fingerprints on the maid's cart."

"Hah!" Letting his panic take the form of anger, he rounded on his son. "And what kind of a place is it where a man can dump my daughter in a basket and go off with her?"

"Daniel." From her place on the sofa beside Justin, Anna spoke softly. She said only his name, but the pain in her eyes had him cursing again and striding to the window. She turned to Justin, putting her hand over his. "Justin—"

But he shook his head, rising. For the first time in the six hours of fear, he knew he was going to fall apart. Without a word he walked into the bedroom and shut the door behind him.

Her robe was tossed over a chair where she had left it. He had only to pick it up to smell her. He balled his hands into fists and turned away from it. The jeweler's box with the earrings he'd given her sat open on the dresser. He could remember the way they had looked on her the night before—gleaming, catching fire in the dim light as she had knelt naked on his bed and held her arms out to him.

Fear and anger rolled around inside him until his skin was wet and clammy. The silence of the room weighed down on him. There was only the sound of rain, falling cold and steady outside the windows. Only a few hours before, Serena had filled the room with life—laughter and passion. Then he'd left her. He hadn't told her he loved her, or kissed her good-bye. He'd walked out with his mind occupied with his own business. Left her alone, he thought again.

"Oh, God." Running his hands over his face, he pressed his fingers hard against his eyes. At the soft knock on the door, Justin dropped his hands and struggled against the sensation of despair. Daniel came in without waiting for his answer.

"Justin." He closed the door behind him and stood, looking huge—and for the first time in Justin's memory —helpless. "I'm sorry for that."

Justin met his eyes as he balled his hands in his pockets again. "You were right. If I hadn't been careless—"

"No." Coming to him, Daniel gripped both his arms. "There's no blame here. Rena—he wanted Rena, he'd have found a way. I'm scared." The big voice quavered as his grip tightened. "I've only been scared once before in my life. When Caine took it into his head to explore the roof and we found him hanging on a ledge two stories up. I don't know where she is." His voice shook again as he turned away. "I can't get a ladder to her."

"Daniel, I love her."

On a deep breath, Daniel turned back. "Aye, I can see that."

"Whatever he asks, whatever he wants me to do, I'll do."

Nodding, Daniel held out his hand. "Come, the family should wait together."

Chapter Twelve

She must have dozed because it was dark when Serena felt herself being shaken awake.

"You're going to make a phone call," Terry told her, then walked over to flip on the overhead light.

Serena tossed her arm over her eyes to shield them. "Who," she began.

"He should have sweated enough by now," Terry mumbled as he hooked the phone in the bedroom jack. "It's after one. Listen." He jerked her arm down so that she could look at him. "You're going to tell him you're all right, and that's all. Don't try anything." He began to dial. "When he answers, just tell him you're not hurt, and you'll stay that way as long as he pays. Understand?"

Nodding, Serena took the receiver.

Justin was on the phone in the first ring. A half cup of cold coffee tipped over on the table and dripped on the rug. "Blade."

Serena squeezed her eyes shut at the sound of his voice. It was raining, she thought dimly. It was raining, and she was so cold and so frightened. "Justin."

"Serena! Are you all right? Has he hurt you?"

Taking a deep breath, she looked directly into Terry's eyes. "I'm all right, Justin. No scars."

"Where are you?" he began, but Terry clamped his hand over her mouth and grabbed the phone.

"If you want her back, get the money together. Two million, small bills, unmarked. I'll let you know where to make the drop. And you'll make it alone, Blade, if you don't want her hurt."

He hung up the phone, then let Serena go. The sound of Justin's voice did what the hours of fear hadn't been able to. On a trembling sob, she buried her face in the pillow and wept.

"She's all right." Justin replaced the phone with studied care. "She's all right."

"Thank God." Anna grabbed both of his hands. "What next?"

"I get the cash together, take it wherever he tells me."

"We'll take photographs of the bills," Lieutenant Renicki stated as he stirred himself from his chair. "One of my men will tail you when you make the drop."

"No."

"Listen, Mr. Blade," he began patiently, "there's no

guarantee he'll let Miss MacGregor go after he's been paid off. He's more likely to—"

"No," Justin repeated. "We play it my way, Lieutenant. No tails."

The lieutenant took a deep breath. "All right, we can plant a bug in the case. That way, when he picks up the money, he might lead us right to her."

"And if he spots it?" Justin countered. "No," he said again. "I'm not taking any chances."

"You're taking a hell of a chance by handing him two million dollars cold," Lieutenant Renicki tossed back. "Mrs. MacGregor." He turned to Anna, thinking a woman, a mother, would be more reasonable. "We want your daughter back healthy, the same as you. Let us help you."

She gave him a long, steady look while the hand in Justin's trembled lightly. "I appreciate your concern, Lieutenant, but I'm afraid I feel as Justin does."

"Photograph the money," Caine put in. "And go after him when Rena's safe. By God, I'd like to prosecute him myself," he added in a savage mutter.

"Then you'd better hope he'll be prosecuted for only kidnapping and extortion—not murder," Lieutenant Renicki added cruelly. "He'll keep her alive until he's got his money. After that, it's anyone's guess. Listen, Blade," he continued as his patience snapped. "You don't like dealing with cops, maybe because you had some trouble years back, but it's a hell of a lot smarter to deal with us than to deal with him." He tossed his hand toward the phone.

In an unconscious gesture Justin ran his hand over his

ribs. No, he thought, he didn't trust the police. The memory of those endless questions while his wound was healing into a scar were ingrained in his memory. Maybe he was making a mistake. Maybe he should . . . His fingers froze abruptly. Scars. No scars!

"Oh, God," he murmured as his eyes dropped to his hand. "Oh, my God!"

"What is it?" Anna was standing beside him, her fingers digging into his arm.

Slowly, he brought his eyes to hers. "A ghost," he whispered. Then shook away dread as he faced Lieutenant Renicki. "On the phone Serena was trying to tell me something. She said, 'No scars.' The man I killed in Nevada put a knife in me. Serena knows the story."

The lieutenant was already heading for the phone. "Do you remember his name?"

Justin gave a mirthless laugh. Did you ever forget the name of a man when you were tried for his murder? "Charles Terrance Ford," he answered. "He had a wife and a son. She brought the boy to the courtroom every day." He had blue eyes, Justin remembered. Pale, confused blue eyes. A wave of sickness rose up, threatening to swallow him.

"This time, drink it," Caine ordered as he thrust a snifter of brandy into Justin's hands.

Looking down at it, Justin shook his head. "Coffee," he mumbled, and walked into the kitchen. But he couldn't think. Pressing his palms down on the counter, he tried to clear his head. Helpless, he realized. He felt the same raging helplessness he'd experienced so long ago in that narrow little cell. Seventeen years, he thought. Dear God, he's had seventeen years to hate me. What will he do to her because of me?

"If it's all you'll drink, then drink it," Caine said roughly as he pushed a cup of coffee across the counter. He was remembering Serena standing there only that morning, her eyes laughing at him while he dealt with the fact that she'd grown up while he wasn't looking.

"I knew," Justin said quietly as he stared into the black coffee. "I knew someone was after me. I knew she wasn't safe, but I didn't make her go."

Caine sat down heavily on a stool. "I've known Rena all her life, loved her all her life. No one, absolutely no one makes her do anything."

"I could have." Justin picked up the coffee and drank without tasting. "All I had to do was go with her."

"And he'd have followed you."

Justin slammed the cup back down. "Yes." The anger cleared his head and dispelled the lingering sickness in his throat. "I'm going to get her back, Caine," he said with deadly calm. "Nothing in hell's going to stop me from getting her back."

"His name's Terry Ford," Lieutenant Renicki stated as he walked into the room and headed for the coffeepot. "Booked a flight out of Vegas five days ago, destination, Atlantic City. We'll have a description soon. We're checking all the hotels, motels, condos, beach rentals, but there's no telling whether he's kept her in town. I wouldn't bank on him renting a room in his own name," he added as he helped himself to the sugar bowl. "His mother remarried about three years ago. We're tracking her down."

It felt good to have something solid to work with—

names, faces. With a satisfied grunt Lieutenant Renicki sat across from Caine. "We'll get him," he promised. "You both should try to get some rest," he advised. "Odds are he won't be calling again until morning." When neither of them answered, the lieutenant sighed. This family knows how to close ranks, he reflected. "All right, Mr. Blade, why don't you tell me what arrangements you've made for getting the ransom together?"

"The money will be in my office by eight o'clock."

Lieutenant Renicki's bushy brows rose and fell. "No problem getting that amount of cash together?"

"No."

"Okay, tell him nine. Then we'll have time to photograph it in your office. That way, if he slips by us, we'll be able to grab him once he starts to pass it. I'd like you to reconsider letting us put a tracer in one of the cases. I can show you how successfully it can be concealed. Remember," he added before Justin could speak, "our primary concern is the same as yours. To get Miss MacGregor back, safe."

For the first time, Justin noticed the fatigue in the lieutenant's eyes. It occurred to him that the policeman hadn't eaten or slept any more than he had himself. Under most circumstances, he would have trusted those eyes. "I'll consider it," he said at length.

The lieutenant only nodded and drained the rest of his coffee.

At six A.M. the phone rang again. Anna and Daniel woke from a half doze on the sofa. Alan came to attention in the chair where he had spent the night, awake and restless. Caine stopped in the doorway of the kitchen where he was returning with yet another cup of coffee. Justin's hand snaked out to the receiver. He'd been staring at the phone for more than an hour.

"Blade."

"Got the money?"

"It'll be here by nine."

"There's a gas station two blocks down from the hotel on the right. Be in the phone booth there by nine-fifteen. I'll call you."

Terry hung up the phone so tied up with nerves, he nearly knocked the small table over. He hadn't been able to sleep even after Serena's weeping had quieted. She shouldn't have been able to make him feel sorry for her, he thought as he rubbed the heels of his hands over his eyes. After all, what kind of a woman was she to be living with a murderer?

His mother would have said she was a tramp, but he'd sensed something about her. Classy, Terry mused as he stretched his stiff and aching muscles. She'd even looked classy in that sweater and jeans when she'd opened the door for him. And last night . . . He sighed, glancing at the door to the bedroom. Last night she'd looked so small and helpless when she'd curled up on the bed and cried.

Well, he was sorry he had to scare her this way, but she was the best weapon he could use on Blade. She shouldn't have gotten mixed up with scum like him in the first place, Terry reminded himself. I'd kill him if I could, Terry thought, but knew he didn't have it in him. Planting a bomb in a building and drawing a knife or

gun on a man were two different things. A bomb was
remote, and he was forced to admit that he'd probably
never have gotten up the nerve to detonate it. But the
threat. Oh, the satisfaction of being able to keep the
man who had killed his father shaking in his shoes.
Then he'd have the money, and every dollar he spent
would be revenge on Justin Blade.

He heard Serena stir and rose to check on her.

She was disgusted with herself. What good had
crying done but to give her a throbbing head and
swollen eyes? She needed to be planning a way out, not
wallowing in self-pity. The arm that was attached to the
bedpost ached and tingled from the lack of circulation.
Shifting on the bed, she tried to rub the blood back into
it. *Think!* she demanded of herself. There's always a
way out.

When the bedroom door opened, her head spun
around. Serena caught the quick regret in Terry's eyes
as he looked at her. God, I must be a pitiful sight, she
thought wearily. Then use it, Rena! a small voice
ordered impatiently. Start using your head.

She allowed the fear to surface again while she clung
to her inner strength desperately. "Please, my arm
hurts. I think I wrenched it during the night."

"I'm sorry." He stood irresolutely in the center of
the room. "I'll fix you some breakfast."

"Please," she said quickly before he could go. "If
I—if I could just sit in a chair. I ache all over from lying
like this. Where can I go?" she asked on a half sob as he
hesitated. "You're stronger than I am."

"Look, I'll take you into the kitchen. If you try

anything, I'll bring you back in here and put a gag on you."

"All right, just please let me get up for a while."

Terry pulled the key from his pocket and unlocked the handcuffs. Serena pushed down the urge to run, knowing she'd get no farther than the door. Clamping his fingers over her arm, he led her quickly through the house.

The shades were drawn. I could be in Alaska for all I know, she thought in frustration. If I could run, what direction would I go? Does he have a car? He must have a car—how else did he get me here? If I could get the keys . . .

"Sit down," he ordered, and nudged her into a rickety chair at the kitchen table. Quickly, he knelt and slipped the cuffs around her ankle and a table leg. Pushing his hair out of his eyes, he rose. "I'll get you some coffee."

"Thank you." Her eyes swept the room swiftly in search of a weapon within reach.

"You'll be out of here by tonight," Terry told her as he poured coffee without taking his eyes from her. "He's already getting the money together. I probably could have asked for twice as much."

"You won't be happy with it."

"He'll be unhappy," Terry countered. "That's what counts."

"Terry, you're wasting your life this way." He looked so young, she thought. Too young to have so much hate packed inside him. "It took brains to plan everything out the way you have. Brains and skill. You could be

putting your mind to so much better use. If you let me
go now, I might be able to help you. My brother—"

"I don't want your help," he said between his teeth.
"I want Blade. I want him to crawl."

"Justin won't crawl," she said wearily.

"Lady, I heard him on the phone. He'd crawl to hell
and back for you."

"Terry—"

"Shut up!" he shouted at her as his nerves threatened to snap. "I've spent all of my life working out how
I was going to make Blade pay. I had to watch my
mother scrimp and save and work in a sleazy diner
while he got richer and richer instead of rotting in a
cell. I'm entitled to the money, and I'm going to have
it." Resigned, Serena dropped her gaze to the table.
"Look, I'm going to fix something to eat. Are you
hungry?"

She started to tell him no, then realized he'd just lock
her back in the bedroom. Instead, she merely nodded,
keeping her face averted while she tried to think.

Hearing him rummaging in the cupboard, she gave
her leg a testing jerk. She wasn't going to get anywhere
attached to the table. She was going to have to take a
chance. When he took the cuff off this time, she'd fight.
With luck, she could surprise him enough to at least get
outside, get someone's attention. If there were anyone
close enough to hear her shouting . . .

When she looked back up, Terry had a large cast iron
skillet in his hand. Without giving herself a chance to
think, Serena moaned and began to slip slowly toward
the floor.

"Hey!" Alarmed, he rushed over, dropping the

skillet beside her as he tried to lift her by the shoulders. "What is it?" he demanded. "Are you sick?"

"I feel faint," she said weakly as her fingers closed over the handle of the skillet. She made herself go limp until his face bent over hers. Using all of her strength, she crashed the skillet against the side of his head. He went down like a stone.

At first, Serena lay still, trying to catch the breath he'd knocked out of her when he'd landed across her body. Then she had a moment's terror that she'd killed him. Struggling, she wiggled out from under him and felt for his pulse.

"Thank God," she murmured as she felt the beat. Quickly, she shifted until she could reach into his pocket for the key. His mother was the one who deserved that blow, she thought as she released herself. Poor kid never had a chance.

Rising, she considered her options. She could run like hell, but the chances were that he'd come to and take off. No, she had to make sure he stayed put first.

Serena stuck the handcuffs into the back pocket of her jeans then began to drag him toward the bedroom. He wasn't a big man, but as she started across the living room, bent over and tugging him by the shoulders, she discovered her strength wasn't at its maximum. By the time she got him through the doorway, she was breathing hard and dripping with sweat.

Resting against the doorjamb, she decided she'd never be able to drag him onto the bed. Instead, she left him stretched out on the floor, attached to the footboard with the handcuffs.

She stumbled on the way to the phone with a

faintness that wasn't contrived. It occurred to her that she'd barely eaten in two days. It would wait, she told herself, shaking her head to clear it. She wasn't about to pass out now. Quickly, she lifted the phone and dialed.

After a quick shower and change of clothes, Justin came back into the living room. Anna was urging Daniel to eat, though she wasn't touching anything on her own plate. She looked up as Justin entered.

"We'll have a family dinner tonight," she told him with a valiant smile. "Rena loves the fuss." He saw the tears swim into her eyes to be hastily blinked away.

For the first time since he had known her, Justin went to her and put his arms around her. "Why don't you go down and speak to the chef? He'll fix whatever you want."

He felt her shudder as her fingers dug into his back. "Yes, I'll do that. Be careful," she whispered. "Be careful, Justin."

When the phone rang she jerked, then drew away. Her face was a mask of control. "He wasn't supposed to call again."

"He probably just wants to make sure nothing's gone wrong." His head pounding, Justin picked up the phone. "Blade."

"Justin."

"Serena!" He heard Anna's quick gasp behind him. "Are you all right?"

"Yes, yes, I'm fine. Justin—"

"Are you sure? He hasn't hurt you? I didn't think he'd let you call again."

She controlled her impatience and spoke lightly. "He didn't have any choice," she told him. "He's unconscious and cuffed to the bedpost."

"What?" Caine grabbed at his arm, but Justin shook him off. "What did you say?"

"I said I knocked him out and cuffed him to the bedpost."

Something rushed through him that he didn't recognize. It was relief. It came out in a burst of laughter. "God knows why I was worried about you," he said as he sunk onto the couch. Looking up, he saw four pairs of anxious eyes. "She knocked him out and cuffed him to the bedpost."

"That's a MacGregor for you!" Daniel exploded, and swung Anna into his arms. "What did she hit him with?"

"Is that my father?" Serena wanted to know.

"Yes. He asked what you hit him with."

"A cast iron skillet." She realized her legs were shaking and sat on the floor.

"A skillet," Justin relayed.

"That's my little girl!" Daniel kissed Anna lustily, then laid his head on her shoulder and wept.

"Justin, could you come and get me?" Serena demanded. "I've had a really dreadful night."

"Where are you?"

"I don't know." As reaction set in, she buried her face on her knees. Don't fall apart, she ordered herself. Don't fall apart now. She could hear Justin calling her name through the receiver and swallowed the tears. "Wait a minute, let me pull up the shades and see if I can get my bearings. Talk to me," she demanded as she rose. "Just keep talking to me."

"Your family's all here," he said, hearing the edge of hysteria in her voice. "Your mother wants to have dinner tonight. What would you like?"

"A cheeseburger," she said as she flipped up the first shade. "Oh, God, I'd love to have a cheeseburger and a gallon of champagne. I think I'm east of town, near the beach. There're a few frame houses farther down the road. I've never been in this section." She bit down hard on her lip to keep her voice from breaking. "I just don't know where I am."

"Give me the phone number, Serena. We'll trace it." Justin scribbled it down quickly as she read it off. "I'll be there, just hang on."

"I will, I'm fine really." Somehow, letting the light into the room helped. "Just hurry. Tell everyone I'm all right, not to worry."

"Serena, I love you."

Tears welled up again. "Come and show me," she said before she hung up.

Justin handed the piece of paper to Lieutenant Renicki. "Find out where she is."

With a nod the lieutenant began to dial the phone. "Knocked him out with a skillet, eh?" He gave a quick, appreciative laugh. "Must be quite a woman."

"She's a MacGregor," Daniel told him, then heartily blew his nose.

"A little waterfront house east of town," Lieutenant

Renicki said a few minutes later, and headed for the door. "Coming?" he asked Justin.

Justin sent him a mild look. "We're all coming."

Serena stood in the open doorway though she shivered in the brisk morning air. It had been less than twenty-four hours, she realized. She felt as though it had been days since she'd seen the sunlight. The grass was still wet from the night's rain. How was it she'd never noticed how many colors there were in a drop of water on a blade of grass?

Then she saw the cars. Like a procession, she thought, and wanted badly to weep again. No, she wouldn't greet Justin with tears running down her face. Straightening her shoulders, she went out on the stoop to wait.

He pulled up in front of two police cars. Even as the car stopped, he was out of the door and rushing toward her. "Serena." His arms were around her, lifting her off her feet as he crushed her against him. With her face buried against his throat, she heard him say her name again and again. "Are you all right?" he demanded, but before she could answer, his lips were fastened on hers.

Why, he's trembling, she realized, and clutched him tighter. As reassurance, she put all of the love and warmth she had into the kiss. "You're freezing," he murmured, feeling the chill of her skin under his hands. "Here, take my jacket." As he started to remove it, Serena caught his face in her hands.

"Oh, Justin," she whispered, and stroked at the lines of strain on his face. "What did he put you through?"

"Here now, let me get a look at her." Daniel took her by the shoulders, then ran his wide hands over her face. "So you took him out with a frying pan, did you, little girl?"

Seeing the red-rimmed eyes, she kissed him fiercely. "It was handy," she told him. "Don't tell me you were worried about me?" she demanded as if insulted.

"'Course not." He sniffed loudly. "Any daughter of mine can take care of herself. Your mother, she was worried."

Lieutenant Renicki watched as Serena was passed from one family member to another. He intended to keep an eye on Justin when Terry Ford was brought out. "We'll need a statement from you, Miss MacGregor," he said, moving over casually to stand beside Justin.

"Not now."

He acknowledged Justin's words with a simple nod. "If you could come down to the station later today, after you've rested." He felt Justin tense, and bracing himself, looked over as Terry was brought out by two uniformed officers. "Easy, Mr. Blade," he murmured. "Your lady's been through enough for one day."

Terry jerked up his head. Justin remembered those eyes. The pale anxious eyes he'd seen every day in a courtroom. He'd been no more than three, Justin thought. A baby. He felt Serena's hand link with his as the anger drained out of him. As they led him to the car, Terry continued to watch Justin over his shoulder.

"I'm sorry for him," Serena murmured. "So sorry for him."

Justin gathered her into his arms. "So am I."

"Some of my men will be going through the house," Lieutenant Renicki said briskly. "If you'd come downtown at your convenience, Miss MacGregor."

"Come on, let's get the girl back," Daniel stated, and took a step toward her.

"Justin will bring her." Anna took his arm and steered him toward the second police car. "The rest of us will go back and plan that dinner."

"She doesn't even have any shoes on her feet," Daniel blustered as he was pushed into the car.

"She'll be all right," Alan commented as he dropped into the front seat. He realized he was starving.

"Sure, she'll be fine," Caine agreed, then leaned over to his father's ear. "I'll buy you a cigar if you go quietly."

Daniel shifted his eyes toward his wife and settled back. "She'll be fine," he decided.

"Come on." Justin buttoned his jacket up to Serena's throat. "I'll take you back."

"Let's walk on the beach." She hooked her arm around his waist. "I really need to walk."

"You're barefoot," he pointed out.

"It's the best way to walk on the beach. You haven't slept," she commented as they crossed to the sand.

"No. But it appears I could have rested easy." He wanted to crush her against him, be certain she was real. Trying to keep his arm light around her shoulders, he brushed his lips over the top of her head.

"I hated to hurt him," she mused. "But I couldn't be sure how he'd react once he had you face to face. So much hate locked up inside that boy, Justin. It's so sad."

"I took something vital from his life. He took something vital from mine." He stopped, holding her close to his side as he looked out to sea. "I'm surprised he asked for such a small amount of money."

"Small?" She cocked a brow at him. "In most circles two million is a hefty sum."

"For something priceless?" He took her face in his hands, then lowered his mouth to hers. Then with a shudder he dragged her close and savaged her lips. "Serena." His mouth raced over her face, coming to rest again and again on hers. "I wasn't sure I'd ever hold you again. All I could think about was what he might have done to you—what I'd do to him when I found him."

"He wouldn't have hurt me." The violence was bubbling in him again, so she soothed it with her hands and lips. "The reason it was so easy to get away was because he didn't wish me any harm."

"No, it was me—"

"Justin. Enough!" She drew him away, and her eyes were suddenly touched with anger. "You didn't cause this; I'm not going to listen to you try to take the blame. What happened today was started long ago with drink and bigotry. Now it's over. Let it rest."

"I wonder why I missed you shouting at me," he murmured, then drew her close again.

"Masochist. You know"—she cuddled against him a moment—"I've had some time to think about our relationship."

"Oh?"

"Yes, I think we need to redefine the ground rules."

Puzzled, he drew her away. "I didn't know we had any."

"I've been thinking." She walked toward the surf, then discovering the water was freezing, stepped back again.

"And?" Wary, he took her shoulders and turned her to face him.

"And I don't think the current situation is very practical."

"In what way?"

"I think we should get married," she said very coolly.

"Married?" Thoughtful, Justin stared at her. She was standing barefoot in cold sand, in a jacket several sizes too big for her, with her hair tangled and tossed, calmly telling him they should get married. An hour before she knocked out a would-be kidnapper with an iron skillet. It wasn't, he discovered, exactly as he'd pictured it. He'd imagined asking her himself when they were in some dimly lit room, alone, warm and fresh from loving. "Married?" he repeated.

"Yes, I hear people still do it. Now, I'm willing to be reasonable."

"You are." He nodded, wondering just what she was up to.

"Since it's my suggestion, we'll settle it your way." Digging in her pocket, she pulled out a coin.

Justin laughed and reached out to take it from her. "Serena, really—"

"Oh, no, my coin, my flip. Heads we get married, tails we don't." Before he could say another word she spun the coin in the air, then snatched it. She slapped it onto the back of her hand, then held it out for him to see. "Heads."

He glanced at it. Dipping his hands into his pockets, Justin raised his eyes to hers. "Looks like I lose."

"Certainly does." Serena slipped the two-headed coin back into her pocket.

"How about the best two out of three?"

A flare of temper lit her eyes. "Forget it," she told him, and started across the sand. She let out a quick screech when Justin swooped her up into his arms. "If you think you're going to welsh," she began, then gave a sigh of pleasure as he silenced her.

"I never welsh," he promised, nipping at her lip as he started to carry her back to the car. "Let me take a look at that coin."

As she twined her arms around his neck, her eyes laughed into his. "Over my dead body."